PENGUIN BOOKS

KATHERINE

Anchee Min was born in 1957 in Shanghai. When she was seventeen she went to work on a communal farm, from which she was later plucked by Madam Mao's associates to become a star of the Chinese propaganda film industry. After the death of Mao in 1976 and the downfall of Madam Mao's party, Anchee Min was disgraced and, with the help of the actress Joan Chen, she left China for the United States of America in 1984. Her first book, the autobiographical *Red Azalea*, was published to remarkable critical acclaim in 1993.

A painter, photographer and musician, Anchee Min now lives in Chicago and Shanghai with her daughter, Lauryan Jiang.

ANCHEE MIN

KATHERINE

PENGUIN BOOKS

PENGUIN BOOKS

Published by the Penguin Group
Penguin Books Ltd, 27 Wrights Lane, London W8 5TZ, England
Penguin Books USA Inc., 375 Hudson Street, New York, New York 10014, USA
Penguin Books Australia Ltd, Ringwood, Victoria, Australia
Penguin Books Canada Ltd, 10 Alcorn Avenue, Toronto, Ontario, Canada M4V 3B2
Penguin Books (NZ) Ltd, 182–190 Wairau Road, Auckland 10, New Zealand

Penguin Books Ltd, Registered Offices: Harmondsworth, Middlesex, England

First published in the United States of America by Riverhead Books 1995
First published in Great Britain by Hamish Hamilton 1995
Published in Penguin Books 1996
13 5 7 9 10 8 6 4 2

Printed in England by Clays Ltd, St Ives plc

TO MICHELE DREMMER

She said that her name was Katherine, Kan-si-ren, sounds in Chinese like "Kill-a-dead-person." Kill-a-dead-person was how I memorized her name.

Names are important to the Chinese because we believe a good name leads to a good life. I liked Katherine's name, because it sounded so strange, so bold, and so ridiculous. My classmates liked her name too. Deep inside us we all wanted to be someone we were not. Katherine represented that to us, starting with her unusual name. Through her we saw a chance to rebel, to be anything other than Chinese. Our lips worked on pronouncing her name, Kill-a-dead-person, Kan-si-ren, Katherine, and the sound brought us satisfaction. It was not a hard name to pronounce, but we had to stretch our mouths into a yawning shape to get the sound right. Katherine, Kill-a-dead-person. It was stimulating. Katherine. We enjoyed saying it. We liked to think that her name smelled of hot blood. We liked to imagine everything that came with the name. A story of the western world.

Katherine said the first thing she would like to know about us was what it was like to grow up during the Cultural Revolution. She said the words emotionally. It made us feel strange because we were taught to despise emotion. We were taught only to say, "I love you, Chairman Mao." Not "I love you, Mama." Never "I love you, Papa." The word "passion" in our dictionary meant devotion and loyalty toward Communism. Emotion was considered poisonous. Since we lost our faith in mankind, our minds had become deserts.

How were we to tell our western teacher that we refused to face what we had done? How could we make her understand that we'd been trying to forget that we had denounced others, fought, and murdered? We said, "It was not our fault." We said that phrase in one voice. We shouted, "Not guilty." The Party said that it was not Mao's fault either, it was someone else's, some lowlife, some whore like Madam Mao, Jiang Ching. She had made our lives miserable. Now that she had been sentenced to death, we would be untangled from her web. We were on our way to great happiness again. How could we explain this nonsense to Katherine?

We could feel the sickness course through our paralyzed bodies. Yet we had to continue to breathe. The Communist struggle was breaking down. *Bin-bai-ru-shan-dao*—Our defeated troops collapsed like a mountain in an earthquake. We tried to build a new life, but all we knew of the world was Russia, Albania, and North Korea, countries that were once our comrades-in-arms. We used to think that we existed only to eliminate them, but all of a sudden we were to be partners with the capitalists. On TV our new leaders wore western suits instead of Mao jackets. The events on TV looked like cartoons, but no one wanted to go to jail, so no one asked questions.

Our newspapers still proclaimed that the globe would not spin without China. "Another good example of a starving person who slaps his face until it swells to pass himself off as well fed," my father would say as he sat on the chamber pot trying to take a hard shit. "The fact is either China opens its doors or the imperialists will push their way in. Period."

"Shut your trap!" my mother said, chopping long beans in the kitchen.

Lying on my bed, I thought about Katherine, the foreigner, one of those imperialists I was taught to shoot.

The East Sea Foreign Language Institute was on the west side of Shanghai, a forty-five-minute bicycle ride from where I lived. The school, established in the great socialist style, was to serve the working class. The Party's Central Bureau required that a portion of the student body be actual workers, peasants, and soldiers.

I was twenty-nine years old in 1982, enrolled in a special work-study English program. Odd days I went to school; even days I worked on the assembly line at the Victory Road Electronics Factory. I earned forty yuan—about five American dollars—a month. The factory employed five hundred workers. We had to wear surgical masks because the air was so polluted. We worked with a toxic chemical solution called "banana water." The government gave us milk coupons as compensation.

I was living again in Shanghai, my hometown, yet I felt homeless. My parents, my brother, and I shared a two-room apartment on Forest Road in the center of the city. We didn't have much to say to each other. We left the house in the morning and returned in the evening like ghosts.

My mother would prepare dinner for us. She would try to cook with as little peanut oil as possible, but still we would run out by the middle of the month. She and my father would fight about how to use peanut oil economically.

My father called himself an ex–shop clerk. In fact, he was an ex-convict. It took the government twenty years to declare him innocent. He didn't get along with anyone and was sick of everything these days. He would either pretend to be blind or deaf, or he would throw a temper tantrum. When he was angry, he would throw cups or shoes at me and my brother. "Go ahead, hit your children!" my mother would yell as she dragged us away from my father. "Kill them—save the government a couple of bullets!"

Sometimes at dinner my mother would try to get my brother to talk and would ask him what had happened on the road that day. My brother was a thirty-four-year-old bus driver. "I wish I had the courage to commit suicide," he'd reply. Or, "I wish I'd run over that fat-assed policeman this morning." Mother would say, "Oh, thank you, Buddha of the Southern Mountain, for another damn good day!" Our father would hiss, "Animals!" Mostly, though, we watched the tips of our chopsticks as we ate.

I pitied my father. He had intestinal cancer. Half his guts had been removed and replaced with plastic tubes. The radiation made him bald. I had a hard time living with him; still, I could not imagine life without him.

My brother and I would wash the dishes and then quickly find an excuse to leave. Once out the door, we would go our separate ways. I never knew where he went and never asked because I didn't want to tell him where I was going. Actually I never knew where I would go. I usually wandered around the streets aimlessly. I would watch people move around the city, feeling numb and purposeless.

Shanghai had a population of fourteen million, a monstrous boiling pot of human dumplings. The streets were crowded every hour of the day. Many were people like me with no room of their own. But others were people who came from faraway villages to look for work to raise enough money to buy fake city residency papers. When they ran out of money, they might be forced to sell blood or children or themselves to survive. Shanghai was a place where desperate people came to risk their lives.

The sweaty smell of a crowd, this is the smell of Shanghai. Walking on the main streets, we had no choice but to rub against each other. This Shanghai was Mao's creation. It represented his ideal China—"power in numbers." Our parents responded to Mao's call to make China invincible and so we were conceived. Because of my mother's poor health, her third and fourth babies didn't make it. My mother was guilty of not being a "pregnant activist."

Since kindergarten I understood that I was one drop in the ocean; I was one of the billions. I grew up learning to walk like a weasel, zigzagging through the forest of thighs on the streets. I wouldn't apologize if I hit others accidentally with the spikes of my umbrella on rainy days; if I had to say "Pardon me" each time, I wouldn't be able to get through the streets at all. Besides, no one ever apologized. People were used to this.

Nineteen eighty-two was a year depression swam through the veins of the nation. "Like a strong arrow at the end of its strength" is how my mother described the Great Proletarian Cultural Revolution. "Can't change *feng-shui*, the course of fate." I sensed that she said it with some relief. She called herself a veteran of the war of living. She said she was ready to surrender. I looked at her and thought that giving up was probably a good idea. What else was there for her to do? She was fifty-four years old and had the face of a bitter melon, deeply wrinkled and drawn. My father too. They looked very, very tired.

The roads were jammed with buses and bicycle riders, waves of pedestrians and traffic police. Everyone yelling like so many dogs barking. After a while I wouldn't hear a thing. The crowd would flow past my eyes like a silent film. Then I would flow with them, feeling weightless, in a washed-out light.

I would stay out until the deepest dark of night, my shoes covered in dust. Thinking about the future depressed me. I was a member of the "stuck" generation: made old by our past, yet too young to surrender to fatalism. After years of devotion to Communism, I am left only with these facts: my home is still as small as a pig shed, the bamboo beds still creak, the chamber pot still stinks, the lines at the markets are still long. Yesterday's reactionaries are still alive; some of them live right next door. They smile at me now—I who used to shout that they should be fried alive and eaten crispy when I was a child wearing a Little Red Guard's armband. Their wrinkled lips whisper in one vicious voice, "Teeth that take root in the land of bitter hearts will grow up to bite the enemy to death." I fear them now.

The map of the East used to be covered with red dots, but now it looks like the webbed, bloody spit of a TB patient. Our old man, the great Chairman Mao, laid out like an ancient mummy in the memorial hall, hiding forever under a crystal tube, took every explanation with him. It was still called the Communist Party and Mao's portrait still hung on the front wall of the Heavenly Peace Gate at Tiananmen Square. But what happened?

"Zebra Wong—Mao's Good Child" was written on the award certificate I won in grade school. I was seven years old and so proud. Tears came to my eyes every morning when I prayed for a long, long life to Chairman Mao.

As a teenager, my greatest wish was to die for him. All the children at school wanted to do the same. We hoped that we would be given the chance, whether it was in Viet Nam in battle against the USA, or on the Soviet border absorbing machine-gun fire in our hot-blooded chests, or even on the street saving a child from getting hit by a bus. Anything. We were willing to do anything to honor Mao.

Sixteen years after the revolution we had to ask ourselves why, when we had worked so hard, so happily, were we now so miserable?

We resented what Communism had done to our lives, but we couldn't escape Mao. We couldn't escape his myth. The only truth we knew was that he had created us. We were his spiritual offspring; we carried his genes. The blood that pumped through the chambers of our hearts was his blood. Our brains were stuffed with his thoughts. Although we were furious with our inheritance, we couldn't change the fact that we would always be his children.

My generation had become disillusioned with the government. Yesterday's glory and honor only brought us embarrassment in today's capitalistic world. We did not have a proper education. The Chinese we wrote read like Mao quotations, the characters we printed looked crabbed and ugly. But how could we forget the thousands of bottles of black ink we used to make posters from Mao's Little Red Book? Our entire youth was written across these posters.

My education from age seven to eighteen was spent learning to be an honest Communist. We worshiped Mao and his teachings. He was like Buddha—we could not expect to understand everything immediately. We believed that if we spent a lifetime studying, we would have a total awakening by the end.

We waited patiently until Mao died on September 9, 1976, only to discover that the pictures blurred with passing time, that the ink on the posters dripped with the wash of each year's rain, that the paper peeled off and was blown away by the wind, that our youth had faded without a trace. We "awakened" with horror, and our wounded souls screamed in devastation. How am I to explain what I have become?

A Chinese saying goes, "If the father is a rat, the son will only know how to dig holes."

We discovered that we were brought up to be double-dealers and we couldn't deny such truths any longer. We learned the art of survival by fighting the war. We learned to distrust; we acted like heartless robots, our souls wrapped in darkness—we asked no questions. We convinced ourselves that tears were only the pee of naughty monkeys.

The Great Proletarian Cultural Revolution was pronounced officially "ended" in 1980. I was now a former revolutionary, a status shared by millions.

Chairman Mao had described himself as a servant of the people, but he was just another emperor. For twenty-seven years he played with our minds. Our heads were jars of Maoist pork marinating in five-thousand-year-old feudalist soy sauce. The spoiled mixture produced generations of smelly rotten thoughts. The thoughts multiplied like bacteria.

Since 1976 we had been singing an elegy for Chairman Mao; now we were singing for our own vanished souls. White elegiac couplets were fluttering in the east wind, covering the entire sky of the Middle Kingdom. The tears of sad ghosts rained down and salted the land, desiccating the roots of spring.

It was at this moment in history, one day in April 1982, that the pink peonies opened their tender lips to kiss the night dew, that grass-green leaves stretched their little hands to touch the soft spring breeze, that she came to us from America.

She was a different animal. Katherine was allowed by the school authorities to behave as she pleased because she was not Chinese. Everyone was watching her. To us she was America. Since 1980 the school had invited a group of foreign scholars to teach, but most of them were old ladies and gentlemen. They didn't talk to the students outside of the classroom—they knew the rules. But not Katherine. She was a newcomer. I wondered how she even got herself accepted by the Chinese authorities. She wrapped herself in vermilion. Her red lipstick made us uneasy. Like an evening star, she appeared quietly in our lives, in complete harmony, and before we realized it, she was installed above our heads. The curtain of night had descended. The sound of humans faded. Air became soft as silk. Lying in my bed at night, I would think about Katherine and her red lipstick. The auburn-haired, lynx-eyed, snake-bodied, beautiful foreign devil.

She pronounced her name twice for us. Katherine something, Katherine Holy-something. It sounded like "good luck" in Chinese. Katherine Good-luck. It didn't matter what her last name was—Chinese never bothered with names that exceeded three syllables. We would just try to use the first three syllables: Kan-si-ren.

Frustrated, she asked the class to translate her name according to how it sounded in Chinese. We smiled in shyness. We wouldn't tell her. But she wouldn't give in. Someone said in a small voice that her name sounded like "Kill-a-dead-person."

Katherine laughed until tears came to her eyes. Such a laugh. A wholehearted laugh, a burst of laughter. It surprised us. No one laughed this way in China. Our hearts beat with strange excitement.

She said the problem was that we did not pronounce her name correctly. The "th" sound in her name should not be pronounced "tsi." We tried hard. Some of my classmates had been studying English for years; they were taught by the same teachers who used to teach Russian. Katherine couldn't understand what they were saying. Finally someone made her understand that we had no "th" sound in our language. "But you should learn to do it," she said. "Because I, your teacher, do not like to be called Kill-a-dead-person!"

We could not take our eyes from her face. Foreign features, made in America. We became fond of, needy for, then addicted to her laughter. She asked us to read. "Choose anything you feel comfortable with," she said.

I recited a poem from middle school. "Chairman Mao, Oh, Chairman Mao, / You are the red sun in our hearts . . ." I stopped when I heard her laugh. She apologized, saying that she couldn't help it. She asked me how I learned my English. I replied that I memorized the sounds by their meaning in Chinese. For example, "the red sun in our hearts" sounded like "big monkey in my shoes" in Chinese. She asked how many people practiced this method. Most of us. She laughed again.

She affected us with such openness. The muscles in our faces began to move like a rippling sea. We began laughing with Katherine, at her, then at ourselves. This was how she started a revolution in our heads—with her laughter.

Our next assignment was to think of a good Chinese name for our teacher. We tried out all kinds of names. We asked our teacher what she liked in nature, plants or flowers? She said she adored peonies. How bold, I thought. I had secretly read the classic Ming Dynasty play *Peony Pavilion* by Tang Xian-zu and the novel *Story of the West Room* by Wong Fu-shi, in which the peony was a symbol of a secret garden tryst, a symbol of noble passion and desire. I wondered if Katherine knew that.

When Katherine asked us how much we knew about America, we replied that it was a capitalist country that exploited its people, although by now we were somewhat doubtful of this. As children, we were taught that people in America wore rags and the children were starving. It made us think how fortunate we were to live in China. After all, we were protected by our Communist Party. We were inside the Great Wall.

Katherine asked whether we had any doubts about Communism the same way we had doubts about what we knew of America.

No one came forward to answer her question. Katherine must have understood the fear behind our silence. "All right, no politics," she said.

I had never had personal contact with a westerner in my life. I had only seen pictures of western people. They appeared threatening to me. "We must learn our enemy's language in order to fight with him successfully" was how Mao's teaching went. It was printed on the cover of our textbook and dictionary. How strange then that this formidable enemy was brought in to teach us.

The Peony, Katherine, was invading our minds. The danger was that we were enjoying it. Our minds had been longing for such an invasion. Coming from America made her a different type of human being. I wondered what her childhood was like. A world filled with fancy toys or a world of starvation? Begging on the streets for food, like the story we were told about the Little Match Girl, who nearly froze to death on New Year's Eve? Were her parents capitalists or proletarians? Did they buy her pretty clothes or make her wear rags and force her to work from a very young age?

She was generous in her interactions with us—I could detect no mental scars that would suggest mistreatment. Her skin was smooth—no weather damage; her back was as straight as a ballet dancer's—no years of heavy labor; her hands were thin and long —evidence of a bourgeois lifestyle. In myself I saw her opposite in every way: the mental scars, the damaged skin, the mark of the past, the rotted mind and chewed-up heart.

Katherine's sweetness upset me and entertained me at the same time. I wanted to ask her: Do you eat dogs or snakes or silkworms? Do you sleep with cockroaches parked on your nose? Why did you pick China? Do you know that just by standing before us you show us how deformed we are?

When she stepped up to the lecture podium, the drama began. We took her in from head to toe. We watched her silently. Thirty of us. Men and women with straight black hair and brown skin.

We wrapped her in our silence. We felt comfortable just watching her. We asked no questions. We let her speak, made her keep talking. In silence we felt in control. We watched her mouth as she said, "Repeat after me please: 'The arrival of a revolutionary upsurge . . .'"

Her hair in the morning was like shooting fireworks against the blackboard sky. By noon her hair became a big red blooming chrysanthemum, its tips curling like Chinese hair never could. When she turned to write something on the blackboard, we took the opportunity to enjoy her thin back and wide, elegant shoulders. Her hair hung down about a foot and it spread like wild seaweed.

"Repeat after me." She paced as she read, holding the textbook in front of her. She came near me. " 'Dead men tell no tales, Comrade Party Secretary.' " Katherine looked up in a curious way, then shook her head with a little laugh. " 'Dead men tell no tales, Comrade Party Secretary,' " I repeated after her. " 'Dead men tell no tales, Comrade Party Secretary,' " the class said in unison. As she read the textbook to us, she opened a new universe.

We heard her but we weren't listening. " 'When one criticizes the doctrine of trailing behind at a snail's pace, the importance of the matter is greatly exaggerated . . .' " she reads as we imagine life in America. " 'Intercourse between Communist parties shall be promoted around the world . . .' " I see a spaceship landing on a strange planet—a glass ball contains a man-made city; inside are people, cars, trains, airplanes moving like toys, giant plants of perfect color and shape. " 'Comrades must bear the brunt of the attack of the nonproletarian influence . . . The better one understands the nature of the obstacle, the less difficult one will find it to be . . .' " Reality intrudes on my dream. Here stands Katherine, who has the exact features of the ones we were trained to kill.

On the odd days I went to work. I hated my job. The noise of the machines beat through my every nerve. By the end of the day my senses were numb. I sat in a dark corner of the factory. I moved like a machine—pick up a roughly molded piece of plastic, bend to file it smooth, flip it over with my fingers, pass it to my other hand to have it cut and drilled on other machines, soak it in a container of alcohol and gasoline, pick it up, stick it under an electric brush to be cleaned, throw the finished piece into a bin, then pick up a new one . . . Eight hours a day.

For the first time the day went faster than usual, because I was thinking about my class and my American teacher. I went to a public bath after work so I would be clean for tomorrow's class.

She liked to wear black. A black dress made from a soft fabric, a black T-shirt with a knit skirt, a black silk blouse, black leather boots. She wound a black patterned scarf around her neck. She stood like a peacock, exhibiting her body, inviting us with her gestures, her body's music and heat. She gave our eyes an indescribable pleasure. As a woman, I envied her. I could hardly stand her.

Officially I was a "borrowed worker" from Elephant Fields—a remote labor camp in midwest China—working for the Victory Road Electronics Factory in Shanghai. I held temporary residence status in the city, because my *hu-ko*, my city residency card, was revoked when I was sent to the countryside to work as a permanent peasant years ago. Non–*hu-ko* workers in Shanghai were classed as "borrowed workers," which meant our future was not secure. Everything depended on opportunity and performance.

When I was eighteen, I was one of the twenty million city youths sent to labor camps to be "reeducated by the peasants," as Chairman Mao instructed. I was sent to Elephant Fields, a remote area with rocky mountains shaped like elephant ears. The city youths were to pick hard, good-quality stones for industrial and military use. The tools we used were no better than what cavemen used. I worked with dynamite.

I lived in Elephant Fields for eight years. My hair turned gray. My memory of the place was worse than a nightmare. I tried very hard to block my thoughts, not to look back. I kept telling myself that I did what I had to, there was nothing to be ashamed of. It was a way to survive. I was too young to know better. And I probably wasn't the only girl . . .

I was haunted at dawn, always at dawn. In the last hour of sleep I would see myself holding a burning stick of dynamite, running through the dry brush, jumping off a cliff, jumping off a speeding tractor, jumping off a tree. I would hear myself scream across the dark, dry land, my breath thick and raspy from the rat poison. I would feel the blood slowly dripping from my nostril, spreading, blooming like a flower on my face, down my neck, a huge red pool on the ground.

Experience had taught me how to live with shame. During the winter of 1979 my village chief, the Party boss of Elephant Fields, felt guilty about what he had done to me and offered to make a deal. If I promised him I would forever shut my mouth, he would try to get me back to Shanghai. He worked very hard, made transactions through middlemen, and at last managed to "lend" me to the electronics factory.

I left Elephant Fields without even a suitcase. I didn't want to take a thing with me, not even my clothes. Anything that could possibly be a reminder of what happened, I discarded.

On the morning of the day I was to leave, the wind was strangely still. No sun. No dynamite. Thick clouds, the same color as the dry land. A giant ant crawled toward me. I stood at the crossroad, waiting for a tractor to pick me up. My thoughts were frozen. I felt as if I had never lived here. I stood still until the ant had crawled up onto the back of my neck and bit me. I caught it in my palm, wished it good luck, and set it down. It crawled up my leg and bit me again. I threw it down and ground it with the sole of my shoe. I looked at the crushed little body and realized that the ant was the symbol of my life at Elephant Fields. With its death I became the murderer of my past.

"Never accept a soft silk sheet for what it is: there might be a lethal weapon hidden underneath"—this was what we learned from the Cultural Revolution. We lost faith in each other. We had been living in spiritual isolation, experiencing the terror of loneliness. We tried to treat this terror the same way we'd treat a mosquito bite—by pretending that it did not exist. I shared my mother's belief in the power of willful delusion: "The heart's eye can see a melon as a sesame seed."

My boss at the electronics factory was an ambitious proletarian. He believed that if the products he made were used in the world's revolution against imperialism, he would be promoted and picked by his Party boss to be a Party congressman. He considered that a great honor and did everything he could toward that goal. One day, while he was reading the *People's Daily*, he asked me if I knew a foreign language. I asked why. Taking a deep pull on his cigarette, he looked at me from behind his thick glasses and said, "You know, English is the most widely spoken language in the world. If you can learn English and translate my factory's product catalogue, I'll try to get you a *hu-ko*—you will be a permanent Shanghai resident."

I could hardly believe he was giving me this lucky opportunity. I told my boss that although I did not know any English, I was willing to learn if he would grant me permission to attend school. When he said yes, I became so charged with energy that I began a "twenty new words per day" self-study program. I tried to figure out everything by myself with a Chinese-English dictionary. I forced myself to memorize vocabulary words without knowing how they were pronounced. Then I would go to the library to ask the correct pronunciation and write it down phonetically in Chinese characters. Soon after, I began the one-year accelerated program.

My boss was pleased with my progress. I had begun translating his product catalogue three days after accepting the assignment. Attending school didn't change my status from "borrowed worker," but there might be a nibble of chance if I did well. I studied and studied, investing everything in hope.

A woman my age was supposed to find a husband. I felt hopeless. I didn't know why. Maybe because of the past. I had no desire to do what was expected of me. Yet deep loneliness made me restless. My heart yearned to reach out but my mind refused.

My brother was engaged to a colleague, a bus conductor. He was waiting for me to move out of the apartment so he could get married and live there with his wife. He would never say this to me, but I knew, I knew what I was supposed to do. After all, I was not the son of the family.

I was expected to make space for my brother. I was to find a man who could provide me with a place to live. Many of my former middle-school classmates had gotten married only because there was a room waiting for them. And this was considered happiness.

I was twenty-nine. I wasn't happy, but I was at least leading a better life than I did at Elephant Fields.

Closing my eyes, I saw myself riding a piece of slippery watermelon rind—I would go wherever it took me.

Katherine was not a strict teacher by Chinese standards. She followed the textbook loosely. She spent half of the class time telling us stories about America. She said that our text bored her to death.

Mostly she spoke slowly in English, sometimes in Chinese that was a little off. She held our attention effortlessly with her absolute charm and her perfume.

None of us wore perfume. It was considered bourgeois. We became wary when Katherine's body carried the smell to our nostrils. We knew we were not supposed to enjoy it, so we all pretended that there was no such smell. But secretly we breathed it in and it took us across the Pacific Ocean to the land of our fantasies. We started to envision smoky images we had never seen before in our lives: graceful, moving bodies of men and women, sometimes naked or maybe in costume, costumes like the ones we remembered seeing in old paintings—paintings the Red Guards destroyed as they looted houses during the Cultural Revolution. We started to hear unfamiliar western music that spoke of secret love affairs. ·

"Mirror. Class, please repeat after me. Mirror." Katherine was teaching us the word "mirror." "The glory of the morning is mirrored in the great lakes of our motherland." We read along with her. "The exhibition mirrors the magnificent achievements made by the socialist revolution and—" She laughed suddenly, then apologized.

We didn't see what was funny. We grew up with these quotations. We would remind ourselves that we were preparing for the revolution as we breathed Katherine's perfume. We were well experienced in holding conflicting notions within the space of our minds. It was part of our tradition: *Zuo-guan-yang-wen-zhang—*

Make the presentation magnificent. Decoration, elegance, and formality held the highest value since ancient times. Still, we were different from previous generations because we were aware of how our ancestors suffered for appearance' sake—they were too worldly, too formal, so they lost *tian-qiu*—God-given pleasure and inspiration. Though we still practiced the virtue of the saying, we were aware that at its heart was a strong, utterly unsentimental disregard for one's inner life.

We were born with our brains cleft. The Red Guard generation was told to forsake tradition, while our grandmothers secretly went to temples to burn incense and muttered prayers to Buddha in their sleep. In a war against honor we were soldiers who attacked traditions that were in our blood. As victors, we could bend them to our needs.

The essence of our belief resided in the concept of the Great Void—above, not a tile to cover one's head; below, not an inch of ground to rest the foot. We were to accept our lives as a vast, ever-changing ocean. The Great Void promised eternal peace and great wisdom. Our grandmothers believed that in it one would feel no terror, only happiness. But tradition had turned my mind inside out and relieved no modern pain.

In the back of my mind I thought that tradition would dictate that I haven't *wued* enough—I haven't understood that one's spiritual life was meant to be lived separately from one's practical life on earth; I was to embrace not-knowing. Still, I had no faith in what the Great Void promised. I didn't want to live the lives of my grandmother and mother. I wanted to think and act with one hand and one head.

I studied her eyes, her pencil-thin eyebrows and velvet eyelashes. We were like fish swimming around her, smelling her and imagining how delicious she would taste.

The men in the class were acting strange. They had a thousand questions, they were suddenly slow learners. They found excuses to ask for special attention from Katherine. Their faces turned red when they were called on to read with the teacher. They couldn't pronounce "Mr. Brown." They said, "Mr. Belong." Katherine would come near and correct them. Smiling like an opening flower, she would say, "Mr. Big Lee, now watch how I move my mouth, it's Brown, Brown, not Belong. Yes, that's right. What about you, Mr. Little Lee, how come you're having the same problem here? It's Brown, not Balloon."

One man would always go speechless when asked a question. He sat two desks away from me. He was tall and thin, with shining black hair pasted onto his skull. A long face, a pair of slanting eyes that rode over a too-small nose, eagle shoulders, a little hunchbacked. His name was Jie-fang—Liberation. Liberation was also a borrowed worker-student. He was from the Hangchou Red Wheat Tractor Factory. Because he was an outstanding worker, the factory paid for him to go to school. I once asked Liberation whether he would go back to the factory after he finished school. "Never, never, never." He spit the words out. I completely understood. He had paid too high a price to get out. "I have been a eunuch for too long. It's time to be a man," he whispered into my ear.

Liberation gave himself an English name, Jim. We all laughed because he made the word sound like "hen" in Chinese. Liberation did not mind. He said he changed his name for Katherine's convenience. We all knew it was a lie. He did it to get Katherine's attention. In a way, we all wanted to do the same thing—change our names. But really what we wanted was to change our lives by changing our names.

There were no good English names that suited the original meaning of my name, Zebra. In Chinese, "zebra" meant "a wild character, a unique spirit." I wondered what Katherine's name meant in English. One of my classmates asked her. She said that it had no meaning, it was just a name. I didn't believe her. How could a name carry no meaning? It was too important a matter to be neglected. Maybe she just didn't want to tell us. Maybe she didn't feel she knew us well enough to explain. I watched her more carefully still.

Jim was a timid mouse in Katherine's presence, but out of her sight he was a bold cat. He told everyone that in his last life he was an English comedian. He told us English jokes. He would explain the jokes and laugh even when we didn't get them. We admired his knowledge anyway. One day he told us that he had learned what Katherine's name truly meant. He said that there were two ways to spell it, either with a *K* or with a *C*, but they meant the same thing. "Catherine" was a philosophical concept meaning "the process of purifying emotion through art." Jim also found in the dictionary a clue as to what had brought Katherine to China. Cathay, a form of her name, he said, meant "ancient Chinese poetry." Jim believed that at some point in the future we would better understand the significance of this discovery.

Jim aroused our curiosity. We all ran to look up "Catherine" in our English-Chinese dictionaries to see if what he said was true. We were not disappointed: "The process of purifying emotion through art." I carefully recorded the phrase in my notebook.

At the same time, though, Jim was having trouble with the teacher. Katherine wouldn't let his problems with pronunciation pass. "Jim, what's happened to your tongue? It's Mr. *Brown.* Say it." Jim rubbed his nose and scratched his head in embarrassment. Katherine waited for his reply. She couldn't understand why he had such a hard time with this no-problem problem. She could never have imagined that the problem was her perfume and her nearness.

After two weeks of class a new student joined us. He came through the door as we were bowing good morning to Katherine. Katherine didn't say anything for a long while; she took a long, hard look at him. Then she said, "Be seated." We all sat down slowly. Her eyes were still on him. She never paid any of us such close attention.

The man was short and badly dressed in a washed-out blue Mao jacket. He carried a green army bag. His hair was a mess. I could barely see his eyes. He introduced himself as "Tian-shi"— Lion Head. He pulled up his hair and smiled. "Sorry, but I was born this way," he said in response to Katherine's stare. "I have this crazy hair, it bursts out like a fire. You see, it's as thick as steel wires. It won't bend. No hairdresser can tame it. My mother says that I must have found my way to the wrong womb."

Strangely, Katherine didn't respond to his smooth English. She said that she had been notified by the school authorities of his arrival. She directed him to an empty chair in the back and said, "We are on page sixteen."

Lion Head went to sit down. He took off his Mao jacket and revealed a red T-shirt. He had strong muscles and a thick neck. He was so ugly, so male. He had a pair of thick, dirty peasant's hands. His huge hands were out of proportion to his body size. He reminded me of sunflowers that grew in the salty land—huge leaves and a little dark-faced flower. His eyes were small—two black buttons in a meatball. His hair fell in his face.

Katherine continued with the lesson but my eyes remained on Lion Head. I read what was written across his T-shirt in white ink: I CLIMBED THE GREAT WALL. He wore dirt-colored trousers and a pair of green army shoes.

Katherine began reading Mao's poem "A Tribute to Female Soldiers":

> A bright and brave look,
> A gun five feet long,
> In the first flush of dawn
> They appear marching toward the soldiers' field,
> The ambitious new Chinese daughters
> Who prefer guns to makeup.

"This is quite a wonderful poem, but is it true that women in this country prefer guns over makeup?" Katherine raised her head from the text and looked at the class. When her eyes met mine, I didn't lower my head like the rest of them. But I didn't answer her either. I couldn't. No one dared make any negative remark about Mao's words. I had only one head on my shoulders and I wanted to keep it. But I liked the fact that she was challenging Mao. I wanted to see how far she would take it.

I heard Lion Head's weird laugh.

Katherine and I turned to look at him. His eyes disappeared, they became two caterpillars. "Of course it's true," he said. "But if you want to learn more about my female classmates, you have to talk to them in their bedrooms." He laughed again. This time we heard a small birdlike sound come from the other corner of the classroom. It was from Jasmine, the daughter of the school's president. Jasmine was dressed like a turkey, in a bright red polyester jacket, tight yellow pants, high-heeled orange-brown fake leather shoes and purple socks with a lotus-leaf ruffled cuff. She always wore fancy socks; it was her trademark style. Jasmine had a small pale face with long permed hair. Her mouth was always in an O shape. No chin. She liked to look at people sideways, as if she were shy. She had Z-shaped eyebrows. She loved it when people told her, "Oh, you look like a foreign doll." None of us had ever seen a foreign doll, but we referred to anything exotic that way. She caught everyone's attention but Lion Head's. Jasmine looked at Lion Head with a pitiful expression. She was staring at him so hard that her O-shaped mouth looked like the spout of a teapot.

Jasmine looked timid but she had the heart of a scorpion. She was "retired" from the military. She was supposed to be a radio engineer but she knew nothing about radios. I tried to befriend her until I learned what happened to a fellow student. A male classmate once was joking with her and called her "Bird Brain." The next day she had her father send this man to a remote rehabilitation camp on the charge that he had "humiliated and attacked a Party member." I was afraid of people like Jasmine. Others said that Jasmine was really as soft as she claimed to be. Today she was soft because Lion Head was nearby. How could you forget someone was capable of such cruelty? You don't send a person to die just because he stepped on your toes.

Jasmine buried her head in her text before Katherine could ask her her opinion. Katherine sighed and said, "Well, I suppose, I have a lot to learn about the inner workings of the Chinese mind."

Lion Head made a big fake nose from flour and put it on during the class break to imitate a western weatherman giving the weather report. He had us rolling on the floor with laughter. Katherine was watching him too. She seemed amazed. Lion Head had always been a fast learner. He told us that when he was ten years old he was sent to a special school to study Russian, French, German, and English because he had a "red" background—three generations of pure proletarians. He grew up by the sea. He loved water and the open air. He ate live lobsters and crabs and never got sick.

Lion Head made everyone in the class uncomfortable. His mind was too slippery to grasp. Except Katherine. She adored him. Smiling, she told him that his English was too good for the class. He said he didn't mind; he just wanted Katherine's permission to sit in. He worked for the government's foreign policy office. He was the district Party secretary's number-four assistant. It was a *xian-zhi* position—a no-job job—like many in the government. He couldn't care less about it as long they paid him his salary. He was even paid to go to school. He came because he liked to chat with foreigners whenever he could to improve his English.

Lion Head and Katherine always had energetic conversations going at break time. The class would surround them while they talked to practice listening comprehension. We grew jealous of Lion Head. He stroked Katherine with his wit. He made her laugh. Most of the time we didn't understand what they were laughing about, but we laughed with them so as not to appear stupid. Somehow they knew that and it made them laugh even more.

Through Lion Head we learned more about Katherine's purpose for visiting China. Katherine was here to teach English, but she was working on a book as well—a research study on Chinese women in the eighties. She explained to us that it was part of her dissertation for her Ph.D. degree in America. She was "playing piano for the cows"—we had no idea what a Ph.D. degree was, not to mention a "dissertation." She said that it didn't matter whether we understood the American educational system. She just needed to talk to people.

She loved to talk to strangers on the street. She was open and trusting. She was foolish. I predicted that she would get hurt by saying the wrong things to people and then she'd get reported. She didn't seem to care. Her Chinese was getting better every day. Every Chinese word she pronounced sounded funny to me, the music off. Still, I liked her confidence, the confidence to confront, to learn, to tackle, and to get her way.

I corrected her accent once when she pronounced *bi-zi*—nose —like *bie-zhu*—crippled pig. She asked if she could pay me to give her private Chinese lessons. I told her with great delight that I would teach her Chinese but would accept no money. She didn't understand that I could be reported as a spy for taking her money. She told me I was being ridiculous. "What are you talking about?" she asked. "If you don't want to accept money, no deal." I said that I couldn't explain any further, because I didn't know her well. How could I know that she wouldn't report me? I would be in trouble if she leaked our conversation to the school authority. I would be labeled as one who "sabotaged the great open image of New China by misinforming a foreign guest."

I was confused when she said that she had to respect my choice. To me it had nothing to do with "choice." It was about the reality of survival.

One of the strangest things Katherine did in our eyes was to rent a peasant's hut for herself. The place was surrounded by rice paddies and was about a half hour by bicycle from the school. It didn't make sense to me that she turned down the offer to live in the university dormitory. Her hut looked primitive; she practically had to shit in a pigpen. Katherine seemed very happy with the hut though. She called it "my home."

Before the semester was over, Katherine said that she would like to invite the class to a party at her hut. The news excited us. We started to plan how we could get permission from the school authority to go. Lion Head suggested that Katherine inform the school authority that she was giving a lesson in American working-class cooking.

The request was granted without any problem. We arrived at her hut earlier than we were supposed to. The sun was still high but the heat wasn't as strong. Katherine had borrowed some straw mats from her peasant neighbor, so we could sit outside. She prepared barbecued chicken with green peppers and onions. Jim and I made an "underground stove." We told Katherine that this was how Mao and the Communist Red Army cooked during wartime. Lion Head went to pick tree branches, straw, and dry leaves, while Jasmine and others came in from the fields with fresh beans.

Katherine said she had a hard time watching the peasants kill live hens. She couldn't eat meat anymore. We waved away her disgust. Jim told her that she would soon get over it. Lion Head said that he would show her how to kill a cat to prepare "sweet and sour cat receiving the worship of frogs." He explained how when frogs were fried their legs extended as if in supplication to the cat meat roasting above. Jasmine said she had already caught a jar of frogs. Katherine said she was going to puke and I thought I heard the sound of her stomach churning.

To distract her I asked why she gave up the convenience of living in the dormitory. She said she liked the countryside and enjoyed the privacy. She said that the landscape and greenery were important to her.

I looked around, trying to see things from Katherine's point of view. There were rice paddies on every side. On the left there was a little pond covered with giant round green lotus leaves. Two big black trees grew out of the water. A bull was taking a mud bath in the pond. Three geese were knotting their heads together, chewing *gao-bai*—turnips. Ducks were chasing each other, fighting over an earthworm. Not far away, peasants were working in the fields. To the right of her hut there was a small path that led to the road to town. Thick swirling dust in the distance meant that a bus had just passed through.

I figured out that Katherine's hut used to be a storehouse for crops. Katherine told us that she had been here for two months and loved every minute of it. She took me to her backyard, where I saw chicks, a goat, and two cats running freely. "This is my zoo," she said proudly. She told me that she had built the fence herself. "I didn't do a great job but it's good enough to keep the animals in." She laughed and told me she loved animals. It made no sense to me. Animals meant food. Why would she waste her feelings on those brainless things? I sneered. She noticed but made no reply.

We sat down and began eating smoked green beans and discussing whether Katherine was Chinese in her past life. Katherine was sure she was.

"So then you must have eaten those animals," I said. "Why not do it again?"

"No! No one is going to make me eat meat!" she said, raising her voice.

"But you said you were Chinese!" I shouted. "Let's prove it."

Jim and Lion Head were laughing and saying, "Dog meat with soy sauce, deep-fried snake with fresh monkey brains, blowfish with pig eyes . . ."

"You're making me sick!" she yelled, and ran away like a child who saw a dead rat on the street. We had fun torturing her, making her beautiful eyes widen. "Do you really eat monkey brains?" she would ask. "I know you're fooling me. Tell me you're fooling me. Teach me some more Chinese!" And I did. I taught her slang, dirty words with double meanings, like how "do an exercise" could also mean "go mate with a pig." She would perform her newly learned phrases in class in an American accent. Everyone would have a wonderful time laughing. Her charm was indescribable. Sometimes she would accidentally forget the word order or tone and the sentence would become "Do exercise a mating pig."

We ate the food she made in her yard. We began to ask her questions. First Lion Head asked a little awkwardly whether Katherine was married. We all strained our necks like ducks trying to hear the answer. Katherine did not seem uncomfortable at all. She said she had been married and divorced. No children. She said she wanted a child though, badly.

We all went quiet. We shot disapproving looks at Lion Head for asking the question. You don't spread salt on someone's wounds, our eyes said.

Katherine's response to this surprised us. "Hey, what's wrong with you guys? It's all right to ask me questions. You don't have to feel bad for me. Divorce is not such a terrible thing. I chose to get married, I chose to get divorced. This is how you learn in life. I've put my past behind me. What's there to be sad about?" She told us to be happy for her, for the freedom she enjoys.

Still, we could not help feeling sorry for her. We had a hard time comprehending what she meant. In China nobody got divorced until a husband nearly murdered his wife or vice versa. We tried to comfort her because we believed she was suffering. We suggested that she try to work things out with her husband. We said, "Don't worry. You can always forgive each other."

Katherine laughed and shook her head. She confused us. "Let's do something other than talking about my broken marriage, okay?" she said. "How about listening to some of my favorite songs?" We all nodded. She took out a tape recorder and stuck in a cassette. She treated the machine roughly. It jammed. She took the tape out and used her finger to clean the inside of the player. She reloaded the tape, patted the machine, and murmured, "Don't you do that again." She smiled as she turned to us. "Ready, class? It's the Beatles!"

"What's Beatles?" Little Bird, a girl with a pair of alarmed eyes, asked. I was glad that she asked because I didn't know what Beatles were either. Jim stood up and gave us an introduction. He asked us if we remembered a story in the Party's newspaper in the early seventies about a group of young western musicians called Beatles—*pee-tou-shi*, in Chinese—men-with-long-hair. The translation itself made the Beatles into a bunch of jerks. I remembered reading the story criticizing them. The newspaper said they were the leaders of "a generation of destruction." I forgot about them because I never heard their music.

"Are they the same *pee-tou-shi?*" I asked Jim. He nodded. Katherine said she was glad to have Jim's information. She said, "Now let's let the music speak for itself."

The sun was setting. The green paddies turned golden. The men-with-long-hair on the tape sang "I want to hold your hand" and the music touched us. Katherine translated the lyrics for us and I thought about my life at Elephant Fields. Tears began to well up in my eyes; I felt glad that I survived, lived to see this day when I could listen to such a song. I saw tears in Lion Head's and Jim's eyes too. What was on their minds? Lost youth or love? Or maybe what could have been? Jasmine was sitting next to Lion Head. She was sobbing silently. The tenderness of the lyrics was like the noontime rays of the summer sun—it touched our icy hearts. It was as if we could hear the sound of ice breaking inside our stiff bodies. Katherine could never understand this. She would never know the impact of this act. I looked at her. She smiled at me with gentleness in her eyes. My loneliness disappeared. We asked Katherine to play the tape over and over until she was bored.

I liked when Katherine called my name in class. She made it sound exotic. "Shao-jun"—Zebra—she made an effort with her tongue. She said that she liked the fact that I was named after an animal even though it was not easy for her to pronounce. She said that it gave her hope that the Chinese were not such big animal haters after all. "Shao-jun, Shao-jun, Zebra." She laughed as she tried to say it again and again. "Am I doing it right?" She made us laugh. We said, "You are doing it perfectly."

After that Friday's class Katherine asked if she could interview me. "About what?" I asked.

"About life as a Chinese woman," she said. I did not answer her. I heard she had been conducting interviews on campus. I didn't want to be one of those people who supplied her, a foreigner, with stories that would please the government.

"People around campus have been enthusiastic about me telling their life stories," Katherine told me, showing me her notebook. The peacock is showing me the jewels on her feathers, I thought. The peacock thought that I cared about her beauty. I decided to pretend to be nearsighted.

"What's wrong with you?" She smiled. Her neck was long and at this moment it seemed too long. I felt crowded by her.

"How much do you think you know about China?" I asked.

"Pretty much," she replied. "I studied for six years and spent a lot of time in a lot of libraries before I ever set foot in China."

I didn't know what to say to her. I am Chinese, and I still don't understand this country. How could she? Six years spent studying books? And she thought she knew China? How laughable!

"What's the picture of China you have in your head?" I asked. She looked confused.

I shook my head, never mind. I said, "What do you want me to talk about?"

"Everything," she said.

"You just don't get it," I said.

"Wait, wait, what did you say?"

I felt tired, but I pitched the ball back at her. "You want me to talk about myself, right? Let me tell you what 'self' means to me. The self, myself, the self as I see it, is composed mainly of selected memories from my history. I am not what I am doing now. I am what I have done, and the edited version of my past seems more real to me than what I am at this moment. I don't know who or what I really am. The present is fleeting and intangible. No one in China wants to talk about his past, because nobody wants to paint his face black. Our past is not a flattering picture, and no one wants to look at it for long. Yet what we were is fixed and final. It is the basis for predictions of what we will be in the future. To tell you the truth, I identify with what no longer exists more than with what actually is. We have lied about what we actually are, and that, unfortunately, will be your book. So would you still like me to talk about myself?"

Katherine looked at me in amazement. She was silent.

I got up and walked away. I heard Katherine tapping her pen on her notebook.

"Hey, Zebra!" she yelled after me. "I thought you wanted me to play you more songs. Would you still like me to do that?"

I ran into Lion Head on my way home. We were both on our bicycles. Lion Head was in a washed-white traditional jacket with grape-shaped buttons, blue pants, and a pair of army shoes. I was in a similar kind of outfit. We rode along the street with willow trees toward the city. Waves of wheat made the early evening a sea of warmth. Just before we joined the stream of bicycle riders entering the main road, a rider in red shot between us.

It was Katherine. She rode like an arrow. She was wearing a red jacket. Her bicycle was painted red. She was gone before we could find her in the crowd.

Lion Head invited me to his home to look at antiques he had recently collected. He lived on the west side in the Pu-Tuo District, known as the "lower corner" of the city. His house was located at the end of a long lane. We walked through a makeshift black market. People were selling clothes, rice, sesame oil, bamboo mats, and kitchenware from displays on the front of their bicycles. The merchants' eyes darted as they made their deals, always on the lookout for a police raid. Lion Head told me that their customers kept watch too. Anyone who spotted a policeman or recognized an undercover cop would whisper to the nearest merchant, "The black bear is out of the cave." In a few seconds the alley would be cleared. The entire market would disappear. When the policemen left, the market would restore itself in no time.

Lion Head's place was on the second floor. His room was narrow and dark, about ten by fifteen feet. No windows. There was a tiny porch in front where he cooked and tended a little garden. He lived with his eighty-year-old grandmother, who slept in an attic cupboard at night. During the day she practiced tai chi and volunteered along with other old ladies collecting tickets at the entrance of public parks.

Lion Head called his place Treasure Island. His neighbors

thought he must be crazy to collect old garbage like "lotus-foot shoes," triangle-shaped, delicately embroidered shoes women wore at weddings during the Ching Dynasty in 1600 A.D.; ceramic tiger-patterned "cooling pillows" that old men used to sleep on in hot summer months; a "kettle of one hundred roses," a man's chamberpot, made from fine ceramic, with extremely detailed carvings and white and blue drawings inside and out. Colorful red wooden masks of Chinese gods and goddesses hung on the walls and dangled from ceiling beams. If not for the noise from the street, I could imagine I had stepped into an ancient time.

Lion Head's ceramic pots belonged to his ancestors in the last century. The only reason these objects survived the Cultural Revolution was because of the political reliability of his working-class family. Not only was his home never looted by the Red Guards, he was able to trade cigarettes for antiques with former Red Guard officers. The pots were so delicate it looked as if they would dissolve into dust at any moment. Lion Head was careful when laying them out. He said his room was too damp. He was afraid that the pots were deteriorating. I helped him lay the pots out on the porch piece by piece to dry in the sun.

He said that he was a self-taught history lover because his hero, Chairman Mao, was a lover of history too. Mao had only an elementary-school education, but he learned everything he needed to be a modern emperor from history and tradition. He studied *The Art of War* by Sun-Tzu. To Mao, people were chess pieces and he was the greatest player. "I admire him," said Lion Head. "He was such a brilliant tactician. He was a free man. He didn't spurn convention, but wasn't going to be deceived by it. This was precisely what made him a hero. He was able to use the dynasty as an instrument instead of being used by it."

When Lion Head talked, it seemed he was talking more to himself than to his guest. He indulged himself and demonstrated his elaborate knowledge of history. He must have felt like Mao at those moments, I thought.

Gently wiping the dust off the antiques, I told Lion Head that I liked to paint and asked him about the ancient way of making paints. He said that they would mix color with egg yolks. It was expensive but good, he said. He painted too, but he preferred photography. He handed me a new jar of paint as a gift and asked me what I liked to paint. I told him I mostly painted symbols, a white mask on a black background, for example, or a giant watch without numbers, a candle burning on both ends, a faceless face. He said that had always been his idea of a self-portrait—a faceless face. He had been trying to capture that image with his camera but hadn't been successful. We sat quietly for a long time.

I told Lion Head about Katherine's efforts at understanding China. He asked if she had seen my paintings. Yes, I told him, I showed her some. He asked what her comments had been. "She said that she saw anger in the paintings," I told him. Lion Head shook his head and laughed.

We talked about Katherine's expectations and whether they were realistic. I told him that Katherine now seemed to understand that she couldn't swallow the Pacific Ocean in one gulp, but she was thinking about taking it one cup at a time, downing it bit by bit. I told him that she intended to capture her experience in the book in units simple enough for her readers to comprehend. She believed she could break it down, like measuring curves by reducing them to a sequence of tiny straight lines.

"That's the thinking of a typical western mind," Lion Head

said. "You see, Chairman Mao ruled China by *not* ruling it. Mao swam in the Yangtze River in the summer, traveled around his kingdom in the autumn and spring, and wrote poems in the Forbidden City in the winter. The basic difference in our beliefs lay in our concept of the Great Void and the westerner's idea of God. They think God exists in the world by *wei*—making—while we believe in the power of *wu-wei*—not-making—which is the *true* creative power."

While polishing and rearranging his antiques, Lion Head continued: "In order to comprehend China, or in fact anything, Katherine must understand that things are not made of separate parts put together, like machines. The Chinese mind doesn't ask how things were made, which to Katherine must sound odd. If the universe were 'made,' there would be someone who knows *how* it is made—who could explain how it was put together as a technician can explain, one word at a time, how to assemble a machine. But the universe simply grows, and the shortcomings of language, for one thing, exclude the possibility of ever explaining how it grows. Katherine must understand that the universe does not operate according to a plan. Katherine is misguided by her western view. She should learn how to open herself to the unknown in order to gain knowledge."

Lion Head's grandmother appeared like a ghost. She leaned on the doorframe. Lion Head introduced me. She smiled, showing the one tooth left in her mouth. She said, "Are you the girl who came last week?"

Her question embarrassed Lion Head.

"No girl came last week," he interrupted her. "That was Jim."

"I am not that old," said the old woman. "My sight is still good. She had long hair. Don't you fool me."

"It's he, not she," Lion Head corrected her.

"No, no, no, I am sure it's she. No boy would wear his hair that long."

Lion Head wrapped up his pots and said to me, "Jim's been influenced by the Beatles, the long-hair-men."

I laughed, thinking how people reacted with shock to Jim's long hair. I thought of Katherine. The Beatles. "I Want to Hold Your Hand." Katherine, the foreigner, the magician.

Lion Head and I ate noodles with eggplant his grandmother cooked on the porch. We looked down at the "mobile market" below. Thousands of heads were moving like ants.

"Do you know why Katherine rides her bicycle in red?" I asked Lion Head as he served me tea. "Is it for fashion?"

"No," replied Lion Head. "She doesn't want to be hit by a bus. Bus drivers in this country are vindictive, like your own brother; there's never a day when they're in a good mood. Katherine is a foreigner. She doesn't care whether people think she's crazy for wearing a loud jacket. She cares about her safety!"

I remember someone in class once scared Katherine by telling her that if she got hit she would be left on the street to die without any help, because life was not worth much in China. She didn't know how to take Chinese jokes. She believed that she would be slipped snake or blowfish if she went to a Shanghai restaurant.

"You just can't convince her that people are just joking with her," I told Lion Head. "She's got a strange mind."

"I wonder what makes an American mind," said Lion Head. "From what I know, they eat cheese as their main meal, and that stuff stinks—it clots the brain tubes you know."

"What exactly did she do, I mean, to her bicycle?" I asked.

"First she painted it red to warn other drivers. Then she had her friends ship a jacket with shiny red strips from America. It looks a lot like the uniform patients wear at the Shanghai Mental Hospital. She's so identifiable when she passes you. She zips here and there like a red dragonfly. Now all she has to do is dye her skin red."

I laughed.

"Her hair color is quite interesting," Lion Head continued. "I would like to touch her hair someday. I doubt if her hair is real. I mean, in America they do all kinds of odd things. I am sure they would mate with animals for money."

We heard the sound of light footsteps on the staircase. Lion Head went out and did not come back for a long while.

I went to check what was going on and saw Jasmine standing downstairs talking to Lion Head. Just by looking at her eyes I knew she was angry at him.

Jasmine did not say hello to me. She stared at Lion Head. In an instant I noticed that her eyebrows looked unnaturally long, as if painted on. I was sure that she had carefully done something to them. These flying eyebrows did not suit her tiny face. Her cheeks receded because of the strong emphasis of the eyebrows. The O-shaped mouth was knotted into a Q.

I dared not say a word.

Lion Head carefully selected his words. He said: "You should be resting. You are too tired. Bad temper produces poisonous chemicals which can harm your body. You must not get upset." With his arm he made a big-brother gesture, patting her on the shoulder. With great tenderness, he said, "Come on, be a good girl."

Lion Head's words did not help Jasmine; on the contrary,

they made her even more desperate. She fixed her eyes on me, and I knew she was seeking an enemy. I could tell she was suspicious of me. The little lips shrank and wrinkled. She began to weep but her anger was strong. Her eyes were saying "He is mine—don't you touch him" with such pitifulness. She made me nervous.

I said, "It's time for me to take off." I went down the steps. I heard Jasmine break down and cry.

One afternoon, three weeks later, on our way back from the library, walking on the early autumn leaves, Lion Head told me about his relationship with Jasmine.

She was her father's doll. Mr. Han was the president of our school and a cadre in Mao's Long March. Jasmine was the old man's life ever since her mother was beaten to death by the Red Guards during the Cultural Revolution as a "capitalist promoter." Her mother was a beauty. Mr. Han wanted every possible good thing to happen to his daughter. He worked hard as the first assistant to the former Party secretary of the school. He was later promoted to president and became the new Party secretary of the school. When he sought a personal tutor for Jasmine, he picked Lion Head, because the young man was bright and humble.

Lion Head accepted this position in rapture. He tutored Jasmine privately three times a week. He taught her English. They spoke broken English to each other with a British accent. She spoke loudly in public; she liked to have people hear that they weren't speaking Chinese. It was their secret language. He never forgot whose daughter she was. He went on spoiling her and in a few weeks Jasmine lost herself in him.

"Are you attracted to her?" I asked Lion Head. After a moment's thought he said that he felt as if he were sitting on the lip of a volcano. He didn't explain any further.

Lion Head never expressed his personal desires verbally, but he always knew what he wanted. He was like a fine tailor whose work is intricate but invisible. His easygoing, bright, and funny personality was impressive to many. That was what got Jasmine, I figured. Because I, deep down, wanted very much to spend time with Lion Head too. He made my dull life interesting.

Each morning Katherine became a fashion model. Unlike us, who wore the same outfit all year round, she changed her clothes every day. We learned American taste from the way she dressed. This morning she was in deep black-green jeans with a tight, sleeveless black top. A belt with a copper buckle around her waist. Beautiful beads, stones, and shells dangled in front of her chest. The outfit accentuated the shape of her body.

We devoured this image in silence. *"Chi-zao-fan-la?"*—Have you had breakfast yet? she asked in Chinese, a little awkward because of our staring.

No one's mouth moved.

"Hey, you! Wake up!" she said, clapping her hands.

We smiled back at her as usual. She knew we adored the way she decorated herself. We knew somehow she did it for us, and she knew somehow we appreciated it. She lowered her head for a moment, then said, "All right. Let's begin our text."

Jasmine was bored in class. She popped sophisticated questions at Katherine. Questions like "How do you comprehend emotion?" She threw around words like "infatuation." Katherine knew the rest of the class was not able to follow. After she answered Jasmine's questions, she would say to us that it was all right for us not to understand everything. What was being talked about was not important, she said. "The important thing is for you to grasp the language, its tone, its sound. Let it roll around in your ears. Catch what you can, do the best you can," she encouraged. Katherine never shut Jasmine up, although I could tell she was irritated.

Jasmine seemed to forget that there were thirty of us in the room. We didn't like her taking all of Katherine's attention. But Jasmine motivated us—we wanted our English to be as good as hers. We wanted to be able to ask questions like hers to Katherine. I never put away my homework before midnight. I studied under the streetlights. I always did well on Katherine's examinations. Katherine was pleased. She encouraged us. After only a few months I was on my way, speaking English in sentences.

I could not remember how long it had been since I stopped communicating with my parents. By the time I biked home, they were already asleep. My mother tried to wait up for me a few times, but I deliberately made it difficult for her by getting home past midnight, until she had grown too tired and had fallen asleep in a chair. I told her the next day that I was in the school library doing homework.

"It's English," I said to her. "It's much harder than Chinese. So don't tell me how I should study." I didn't tell her I resented that I had no private space at home. I could not invite Katherine over to my place the way Lion Head could. I had no friends. I was twenty-nine. I had a heart, but no one to share it with. Inside, my loneliness was burning me down to ashes.

My brother was seeing another girl. His bus-conductor fiancée had deserted him for another man because my brother couldn't get a room of his own. My mother found a letter under my brother's pillow to someone named Little Lily. He wrote, "Let's meet in People's Park tonight at seven." My mother was excited when she showed me the letter. She asked me whether I knew Little Lily and whether she was a nice girl.

I said that I didn't know the girl. Maybe she was the nurse at the hospital who tended my brother when he became sick over his breakup with the bus conductor. In any case, whether the girl was nice or not was not important, I told my mother. The important thing was my brother had to have a room in order to keep this relationship.

"Why have kids if you have no place for them at home?" I said to my mother angrily and immediately regretted what I had said. Mother didn't say anything. She lowered her head and walked out of the room. Her feelings were hurt. But how was I to stop myself from being miserable?

My brother made me feel hopelessly old. He was thirty-four and could wait no longer. He tried not to speak to me. He beat me with his silence. Every day. Every night. I cried, but without tears. There was nothing interesting in my life except my English class, except Katherine and her music.

I looked at myself in the mirror in the bathroom we shared with neighbors. Let the neighbors' kids pee in their pants, I thought to myself, and locked the door. I remembered something my grandfather once told me. He said our great philosopher Chuang-Tsu taught us that a perfect man uses his mind like a mirror. It grasps nothing; it refuses nothing. It receives but does not keep. My grandfather was trying to guide me toward the

Great Void. But I felt like I was born with a defective brain. I was incapable of being a perfect mirror. I kept what life showed me. I saw myself aging in my own mirror. I was aging faster than I was prepared for. How could I make things happen for me before it was too late? Do people in America live differently? Katherine looked cheerful. She must be at peace with herself. How did she do that? She had a healthy, unclouded smile, an interest in other people. Was she treated nicely in America? Why did she come here? What was it about China that attracted people like her?

Chinese Women in the Eighties. I thought of the title of Katherine's future book. What was there to write about? Our shame? What if my brother decided to marry Little Lily before the new year? He would take her home and get married in my bedroom. Where would I go?

Katherine gave the class a tip about dressing. She said if you have nothing to wear, wear black. The following Monday every one of us was wearing black. Black blouses, black pants, black shoes, black socks. It was ridiculous, the whole class, as if we'd dyed our clothes black over the weekend. At first we tried not to show our embarrassment. We tried to pretend that it was just a coincidence.

I said to Lion Head that I had to wear black because I had a funeral to attend. Lion Head said he had to wear his black suit because it was his grandmother's wish. He said that it was made of good fabric, and it had been sitting in the suitcase for so long the moths were beginning to eat it.

We were fine until Katherine stepped into the room. She opened her mouth halfway and then began to laugh. She laughed and laughed and bent to the floor. She said, "You guys really have a great sense of humor."

We laughed with her. She was in a bright red cotton dress. She said red went well with black. She took out a camera and said she wanted a picture of us. Lion Head offered to be the photographer. He placed Katherine in the middle. Katherine put her arms up in the air. Lion Head stood on top of the lecture table and aimed the camera at us. "You look like a giant black flower with a red heart," he said, and pressed the button.

Without warning, Mr. Han came to supervise the class. Everyone knew that Mr. Han was Jasmine's father, but he pretended that he was nobody's father. He entered the classroom cold-faced. He nodded at Katherine and came into the room with marching steps.

Jasmine sat in the corner where she could keep Lion Head in sight. When Mr. Han passed his daughter, no greeting or change of expression passed between the two. Mr. Han sat in the last seat in the far corner.

The classroom became so quiet that we could hear the sound of Katherine's chalk scratching on the blackboard.

Mr. Han was a big northern man with a potato face and a pair of fearful eyes. He had a wolflike stare and a face full of cysts. Jasmine once told us that the doctor of traditional medicine had said that her father had too much "fire" in his body, that he ate too much ginseng in an effort to prolong his life. When Mr. Han was happy with something, he would laugh loudly and pick his nose. He always picked his nose in public and it embarrassed Jasmine. She said that since her beautiful mother died her father reverted to his old peasant habits—picking his nose, blowing it with his hand, and wiping the snot on whatever he could reach—

wall, tree trunk, or door—and squatting on a bench like an owl when he ate. He said Chairman Mao used to squat when he ate during wartime.

When Mr. Han was unhappy, he would try to control his temper by using his tongue to remove a gold tooth and sucking on it loudly. Once in a while when he was really upset, he would distractedly take the tooth out with his fingers, wipe it on his shirt, and put it back in. Everyone tried to keep their distance from him.

He sat with us and we became other people. We became the tight screws that ran the Communist Party machine, rotating the way we were supposed to. We sat with our backs straight. The class looked like a still photograph.

Katherine was affected by our fear. She grew nervous. She sensed that Mr. Han was a sign of danger. She began to teach "The Communists are the hope of the world's tomorrow." Everybody read after Katherine clearly.

I felt like there was a secret code between Katherine and us. Because Katherine did not like the textbook, she printed her own material for us. Stories of America, mostly about the way she grew up, her family, her friends, her neighbors, and her experiences. We almost forgot our official textbook.

But in front of Mr. Han we pretended that we had no interest in Katherine. We acted one hundred percent Communist.

Jasmine didn't seem to like that her father came to class. She put her face in her palm and napped throughout the session.

Our school used to be a rich man's summer palace before the Liberation. Behind the brick building, a hundred yards away, there was a pond where the concubines used to drown themselves. It was covered with green, wild plants, and thick ivy. It was cool in the summer. In the morning, fog would drape over the pond, bringing smells of dead animals. Beyond the pond there was a small area of forest. It was called the Forest of the Concubines. The trees had no bark. They looked like naked bodies at night.

As students, we were allowed to come to the pond to study our vocabulary. But secretly we came to digest what Katherine fed us. Here we fantasized about Katherine's life, and here we dreamed of being Americans.

In late autumn Katherine got permission to take the class to "do revolutionary research" on a southwest mountain area—an old Red Army battleground, a revolutionary landmark. When Katherine announced the news, no one cheered, because we could not believe it. The idea of travel was so closely related to bourgeois luxury. We dared not dream about such a trip. But Katherine made it a reality.

When the news sank in, we sat around discussing our plans. We had nothing else on our minds but Katherine and the mountains.

I worked three night shifts in the factory in order to receive permission to take a long leave. I was too excited to sleep the night before the trip. Lion Head called for me outside my window at four-thirty in the morning. He said that he wasn't able to sleep and had already packed his stuff. I told him that I had finished my packing too. "What are you waiting for? Let's go," he said.

Lion Head and I sat by the pond near the school. It was five o'clock in the morning. The day began to break. We wore rubber boots to protect our legs from mosquito bites. Wild geese sang their morning song in the dark. Lion Head picked up a stone and threw it into the pond. The sound echoed deep in the forest. We began to talk about the concubines. Lion Head said that he imagined them to be very beautiful. "Look at those skinless trunks—the surfaces seem so smooth," he said.

Lion Head asked me if I were afraid of ghosts. I said I didn't believe in them. "Well, what would you do if they came to get you?" he joked.

"I would shoot them," I said. "I would shoot them the way I was taught to shoot American imperialists."

Lion Head sighed. He said that he too thought often about the way he was taught to shoot American imperialists. "Were you good at target practice?" I asked.

"I'm a crack shot," he replied. "I had six years of training." A smile began to play around his mouth.

I said, "I bet I know what's on your mind."

"Take a guess," he said. "Let's write down the first letter of what we're thinking, in English. We'll see if we're thinking about the same thing."

We pressed our fingers into the mud. I made a K. I leaned over to see what he had written. It was a K too.

The dew wet our clothes. The sun began to rise. The clouds were turning red. I suddenly thought that it would be bad for someone to see me and Lion Head sitting here together so early. We could be charged with a crime—an unmarried man and woman spending the night together. "What if someone sees us here?" I asked.

"Don't worry. We're not doing anything. Jasmine will be our witness," said Lion Head.

"Jasmine?" I looked around. "Is she here?"

"Somewhere. Hiding, I believe. I called her before I called you," replied Lion Head. "I asked her to come down here and told her where we'd be."

I turned to look at Lion Head. I could not see his eyes quite clearly. I asked what he thought of Jasmine. He said he didn't like to discuss one woman in front of another. I said I respected him for that.

He said he could not play games with me, because I knew he was full of shit.

Lion Head began his confession. He said that he thought Jasmine was nice but not attractive. This shocked me. He believed she was boring because she didn't know how to carry herself. "She is a soulless body," he concluded.

Do I have a soul? I asked myself. Images of life at Elephant Fields began to emerge—the dynamite, the smoke, the sound of an explosion, the rain of stones, the heavy breath of a man . . . I shut off my thoughts.

Lion Head turned to look at me. Slowly he got up and began to wander around the pond.

I forced my thoughts back to Jasmine. She was an interesting character to me though not to Lion Head. She had no self-confidence in front of Lion Head because he had destroyed it. Unfair as it was, she actually believed that she was worthless. Not being able to please Lion Head frustrated her. She embraced the torture. She was addicted to it. When they were together, I saw pity on Lion Head's face. He wore an expression that said, How can I kick a dog that has already drowned? He let her know that he would give her no happiness. He expressed this through boredom. He would say, "Jasmine, what's wrong with you? You're not my slave." He would say things like that in public. And Jasmine would sob her eyes out and then plead with him in private, in front of her father, forcing him to apologize. She would tell him over and over that she could not be happier being his slave.

Jim was furious about Jasmine's attitude toward Lion Head. He called them "a fresh rose misplanted on bullshit." He spoke to Jasmine of her stupidity. He pointed out Lion Head's game. Jasmine admitted her love addiction but said she could not help herself. She said Lion Head carried her soul. Without him she would be a walking skeleton.

I asked Lion Head his idea of an attractive woman. He said that I should ask Jasmine. "Jasmine knows my opinions about women."

Morning finally cut through the fog. Jasmine showed up in a brown outfit carrying a basket. As her small figure approached, I thought of how long she must have been waiting in the dark.

Jasmine brought Lion Head steamed breads. Lion Head motioned to her to pass one to me. Jasmine offered the basket my way but she was not pleased.

I watched Jasmine as she watched Lion Head eating. A woman in deep desire. I was moved by her. A soulless body. Lion Head, the short man, was the master who owned Jasmine's soul. Jasmine had the eyes of a female animal during mating season. She stared at Lion Head as if her purpose in life was to attract him. But he had nothing more to do with her after he finished the food. He got up and went to greet other classmates as they began to show up.

Jasmine stood under a tree with her empty basket. She wiped her face with the cloth Lion Head had used to wipe his hands.

At seven-thirty Katherine arrived. She wore flowery cotton pants with a yellowish short jacket and matching leather shoes. The spiky top of her hair was brushed forward in the shape of a chrysanthemum. She carried a huge black canvas bag. I forgot about feeling sorry for Jasmine.

I went up to Katherine and said good morning. "Who will be our tour guide to the mountains?" I asked her.

"Jim will be our leader," said Katherine. "He lived there for seven years as a city youth in a reeducational program during the Cultural Revolution. Is he here yet?"

After Lion Head said hello to Katherine, he turned to me. He was smiling at his own thoughts. I asked him why he was smiling.

"You two look good together," he said. "You and Katherine."

"I wish I wore something that wasn't black," I said.

"No, don't change anything," said Lion Head. "I like the way you two dress. You complement each other."

"The harmony of our colors?" I asked.

"I'm not sure," he said, and went to give a cigarette to the bus driver.

I noticed Jasmine staring at me. She was in love with her hatred. She was shredding her basket to pieces.

When Jim arrived, everybody cheered. The bus driver closed the door. It was such an old bus that he had to kick it into gear. In thirty minutes we were out of Shanghai.

Lion Head waved Katherine over to sit beside him. Before she had time to react, Jasmine took the seat. Katherine smiled and took the empty seat next to me. Lion Head leaned forward and asked Katherine if he could borrow her tape player. Katherine lent him the machine and a set of headphones.

Lion Head never took the headphones off his ears the entire trip. He was punishing Jasmine for possessing him.

Jasmine chose not to react. She looked out the window.

I asked Katherine her impression of Chinese women so far. She said the more she studied, the more she was confused.

"They don't seem to mind the interviews," she said, "but they never tell the whole truth. They have this image of themselves and they want me to buy into it. It seems the only form of communication is speaking about the surface."

"No one tells the truth here," I said. "You have to figure out where to find the truth."

"Where?" She was eager.

"Have you read the novel *Dream of the Red Chamber*?" I asked.

"You know, I tried, but to tell you the truth, I didn't really like it. It dragged on too long. The characters spent their lives playing mind games."

"That's exactly what China is about," I said. "Fabrications. Mind games have been the essence of this culture since ancient times. The way to figure it out is to quit thinking about it. 'A wise man makes provision for the stomach and not for the eye,' which is to say that you can only feel the truth. Like how trees show the form of the wind, and waves give vital energy to the moon. You will never be able to physically locate the truth. You have to judge by the concrete content of your experience, and not by its conformity with purely theoretical standards. It is a skill that would be blocked if you tried to master it with western methods and techniques."

I recited an ancient poem to her.

> The centipede was happy, quite,
> Until a toad in fun
> Said, "Pray, which leg goes after which?"
> This worked his mind to such a pitch,
> He lay distracted in a ditch,
> Considering how to run.

Katherine blinked her eyes with her unusually long eyelashes. I remembered then that I once had a dream about her eyelashes. They turned into bushes, the earth's eyelashes.

Katherine turned to me and said that she found conversations with me inspiring. She asked if we could talk more. I told her that I did not wish to be interviewed. She asked why and said that sometimes I confused her in a strange way.

I suggested we learn from the centipede, let things take their natural course.

Persimmon Village was an extraordinary place in the mountains. Extraordinarily poor and extraordinarily beautiful. The villagers wore rags, and their houses were primitive-looking, mostly made of granite stones. The village was surrounded by persimmon trees and strange-looking plants the villagers called "soap trees." Soap trees had brown leaves and bore half-moon-shaped, peapodlike fruits. When the fruit ripened in autumn, the children would shake them down, collect them, dry them, and put them in baskets to be used as soap. The villagers didn't believe in the kinds of soap we used. They bathed their children with soap-tree fruit and washed clothes and dishes with it. The fruit had a wonderful smell, almost like lilac.

The villagers were full of warmth. They made their living by growing tea trees and selling dry persimmons. They had hardly seen city people before. They sent their kids to bring us home-made sweet potato chips and dry persimmons, food they stored for the New Year celebration. In return, we gave the children gifts of fancy notebooks, pencils, and colorful nylon bags. The villagers let us use their elementary-school classroom as our base.

In the evening, with a cup of fresh tea in hand, we went to sit on a mountaintop that overlooked the village. It looked like an ancient Chinese painting, with streaks of gray smoke coming out of the chimneys. We smelled the soap-tree fruit and watched the villagers being greeted by their children as they returned from the day's work with hoes and other farming tools on their shoulders. Laughter and singing filled the air.

It was here we learned more about Katherine, the girl from Michigan, America. We walked back to the playground of Persimmon Village Elementary School and Katherine showed us her cartwheels.

We watched her with fascination. It was not the way she did the cartwheels that surprised us, it was our own lack of imagination: none of us had expected her to have the movements of a deer, and to turn cartwheels like a professional gymnast. Katherine finished before memory's claw had a chance to grasp the image. We dared not ask her to do it again. We were afraid she would say that she hadn't done a thing, that it had all been our imagination.

"Hey, what's wrong with you?" Katherine shouted. "It wasn't that bad, was it?"

Our curiosity soared. We asked, in broken English, where she grew up, how long it took her to learn to do cartwheels, and who was her master.

She laughed, then she told us about how her hometown was "surrounded by oak trees." "We sold our old house and bought a new one with a big backyard in the sixties. My parents preferred the suburbs to the city . . ." The lake, she said, was called Lake Michigan. "The lake was the real reason our family chose to move there. I love to smell the air and listen to the sound of waves at night . . ."

Her words were incomprehensible to us. We had no notion of such phrases as "preferred," "chose," or "bought a house." We believed that we were wild seeds; we grew and died where the wind dropped us. It never occurred to us that we had a choice in life, that one could do what one "loved" to do. We were never asked what we "preferred" or what we would like to "choose." We never thought that a house could be "sold" and "bought." We began to see what we had missed in our lives and understand what it meant to sacrifice individualism to serve the ideals of the group.

As we learned about Katherine's life in Michigan, America, we began to taste something that had a sweet-sad taste.

She said that she did not know her biological father, had never seen him. Her mother was born blind and deaf. When Katherine was six weeks old, her mother was told by a neighbor that the child had been crying for hours; the mother could not hear a thing. The mother was afraid that the baby might fall ill at night and she would be helpless. She made the decision to give her up for adoption.

Katherine was two months old. No one could be sure whether she would turn out to be deaf in the future. But she was a healthy baby, strong-limbed, with a pair of clear, dark brown eyes. She would raise her little hand and watch it with fascination. She turned when the nurse clapped her hands. She seemed to have perfect senses.

A Jewish family adopted her. The family already had a handicapped child. If Katherine turned out to be blind or deaf, she would not feel too isolated. Her adopted father was an auto-factory worker and her mother was a grocery-shop clerk. With both parents working, she spent most of her spare time in the backyard garden rocking her dolls, observing the growth of flowers, and chasing lightning bugs, forever waiting for her parents to come home.

A little girl, playing with her dolls in a garden. I began to see the picture. I could also picture myself, wearing shoes with the soles falling off, walking the streets on a rainy day, collecting pennies for starving American children. I could see the young Katherine singing songs, visiting an imaginary zoo in her backyard, and I remembered how I had to kill my only pet—a hen with the reddest crown—to heed Mao's call to abolish disease in the city and prove one's loyalty. I listened to Katherine talk about her loneliness as a child, and I thought of how many nights I was left waiting at the gate of my day-care school, the last one to be picked up, waiting for my parents to finish their shifts, and the times they never showed. The images mixed, superimposed themselves on each other, and her tears became mine, and mine hers.

Katherine spoke about forbidden subjects, about Christmas, and the American tradition of family gathering; about her idealistic dreams of a peaceful world—she once filed an application to join the humanitarian Peace Corps; about desire, love, and passion—her fascination with a neighborhood boy when she was sixteen, he seventeen.

On a full-moon night, under a big oak tree, the young man and woman found their passion unstoppable. They fell in love. The young hearts cared not about money, class, boundaries. Be together or die, this was their only thought. The boy secretly climbed into Katherine's room and they took each other in their arms and their bodies became inseparable. "He was so tender and so gentle. We kissed and kissed, held each other all night. We fell asleep with tears of joy on our faces. God, I can't believe it was so long ago . . . It was like a song, a movie, a poem, it always stays with me, reminding me that there are beautiful things in life."

Our cheeks became feverish as Katherine's voice grew soft. We dipped our hearts in its sweetness. Our class began a love affair with her, a love affair that would seek to reclaim the land of our hearts.

In many ways my relationship with Lion Head began on our way back from the mountains. We spent three days in Persimmon Village living with peasants and learning to love the Chinese landscape. We bathed with soap-tree fruits that made everyone smell like lilac through and through.

The trip with Katherine lightened our spirit. On our way back on the bus, I couldn't help talking to her. My mouth was like an open dam, thoughts rushed out. I asked her many questions, including questions I would never ask a Chinese: about men, about what kind of men she found attractive. It surprised me when Katherine said that she considered Lion Head attractive. From that moment on, Lion Head was a different man in my eyes.

Katherine said that an attractive man was someone who was sure of himself, acted on his own will, and had style. I looked at the men around me and I figured that Lion Head was the one who most closely fit the description. He did have a certain weird style.

Katherine said that she had had a dream about Lion Head in which she had slipped into Jasmine's role. She said it was a "hot dream." I asked her to explain. She said, "Hot. A sexy dream." She laughed.

I looked at her and began to wonder, Did she mean that she

felt desire for Lion Head? I turned to look at Lion Head, who was lying in the back of the bus, sleeping like a baby. His expression was peaceful. The face reminded me of the angel Katherine described in her Christmas stories.

Through Katherine's imagination I found Lion Head irresistible. I began to think his eccentric laughter charming, his talk enlightening. I began to think of this boy-man as the Son of Light; wherever he went, the place shined, flowers bloomed. His arrogance nurtured my desire. I started to see why Jasmine refused to let him go.

I got Lion Head more old urine-colored traditional paintings from my neighbors. He was very pleased with my "sharpening taste." In return, he gave me all the dry soap-tree fruits he brought back from Persimmon Village. He said he loved the smell. Every time I visited him, he insisted on smelling my neck. He said he had became a "soap-tree man." "Jasmine ran out of soap-tree fruit, and her father was mad at me for not providing it for his daughter." One day Lion Head told me that Mr. Han had had a serious talk with him. He made sure Lion Head understood the power Jasmine held over his future. Mr. Han painted a picture of what might happen if Lion Head continued to neglect his daughter.

Lion Head told me that he considered himself a free spirit. To imprison him was to bury him. He tried to dance around the president's "mousetrap." But Mr. Han was no fool. He had warned Lion Head that there were rules that could not be broken and boundaries that must not be crossed. "I might break Jasmine's neck if that old fart pushes me one more inch," Lion Head said.

Lion Head made up his mind as he talked to me. He decided
to surrender to the president's power, but not live in misery. He
said that he would enter a spiritual realm, where he would be
his own master. He believed that the path of liberation was a
progressive disentanglement of one's self from every form of iden-
tification, to realize that one was not this body, these sensations,
these feelings, these thoughts, this consciousness. He explained
that the basic reality of life could thus be altered.

"In order to grow," he said, "I must cease knowing. I am the
Possessor of Knowledge, and the Possessor of Knowledge can
know other things, but cannot make himself an object of his own
knowledge, in the same way that fire can burn other things, but
cannot burn itself."

I had trouble understanding Lion Head. One minute he was a
driven man in pursuit of his goals; the next, he was an aimless
wanderer. While he flooded me with his philosophy, he made
complete sense. But when I went home and thought about it, his
words contradicted his actions. On the one hand, he presented
himself as a helpless puppet of circumstance; on the other, he
proclaimed he was in an ideal stage of his life, where he was free
of all boundaries, like the Zen image of the moon in the water, a
phenomenon likened to human experience. The water was the
subject, the moon was the object. Without water, there was no
moon in the water, likewise when there was no moon. When the
moon rose, the water did not wait to receive its image, and when
even the tiniest drop of water was poured out, the moon did
not wait to cast its reflection, for the moon did not intend to cast
its reflection, and the water did not intentionally receive its
image.

Lion Head spoke so freely about concepts like the moon in

the water. He said he was a man who "begins with ease, was never not at ease, was unconscious of the ease of ease."

Lion Head would bring Jasmine flowers during the day and invite me to his place at night. He'd take me to the park and we would walk around in the dark for hours. He'd speak about Jasmine and her vicious father. He'd calmly talk about survival and his ambition of becoming a hero of his time. He said that Jasmine used her pitifulness to get what she wanted. The truth was that she never gave in. She always won. She made the others feel guilty and eventually they surrendered to her. She had gotten her way ever since she was a little girl. There was poison in her tears.

"But she will never have me to keep," Lion Head said firmly. "I am nobody's concubine."

I admired him. In his unswerving spirit I discovered a desire to share his risk and offered him my protection.

One evening Lion Head had liquor in his room. He put the antiques in the corner and sat on his bamboo bed. He lay down and had me sit on a wooden chair next to him. There was a square table alongside the chair with a dim lamp on it. Books filled the shelves and were piled on the floor; his clothes hung on the back of the door.

We faced each other, two feet apart. I could smell soap-tree fruit. His eyes were shining. He asked me if I knew what today was. I suddenly remembered that it was the day of the mid-moon. He poured me a cup of liquor. I said I didn't drink. He said just a sip. We toasted.

The antique clock was noisy. It sounded like a dying windup toy. The liquor felt good. My cheeks burned. Nothing mattered.

Lion Head said he had made sweet-and-sour vegetables and pick-les. It took him three days to prepare. "On the first day, you salt the chopped vegetables," he said. "Second day, you wash off the salt and dump the vegetables into a jar filled with vinegar and sugar, and close the lid tightly. Third day, you add more vinegar, stir the vegetables, press them tightly against each other, and let it sit. When it's ready, it should taste sour-sweet and crispy."

I chewed the vegetables. I heard the crispy sound. I sipped more liquor. My head felt light, my blood running fast. He reached out and his finger touched my cheek. "You are an ancient goddess tonight," he said. He asked if I cared to hear him recite an ancient poem by Li Ching-chao. I told him that I knew all about Li Ching-chao. "I love her poems."

"That's very good," he said. "Let's recite one together."

> The fragrance of the red lotus fades,
> And the bamboo mat is touched by autumn chill.
> I loosen my thin robe
> And board the orchid boat alone.
> Who sends this elegant letter through the clouds?
> As the wild geese return in formation,
> Moonlight fills the western chamber.
>
> Petals are falling, waters flow.
> One image of love,
> Two places of separate sorrow.
> There is no way to banish this feeling.
> As it leaves the eyebrows,
> It enters the heart.

Lion Head suggested that we go to Wolf Teeth to celebrate the mid-moon. It was four hours by bus from the city. There was an ancient altar down by a cliff. Superstitious people went to Wolf Teeth to pray for deliverance.

We arrived at Wolf Teeth just before midnight. We brought a flashlight but did not use it—the moon was bright enough to see the road. Long wild bushes had grown over the altar. We sat by it and felt like we were sitting in a womb. I looked up and saw the wolf-teeth-shaped cliff outlined in the moonlight. The thick mountain plants dangled down like God's beard. We heard the sound of a waterfall beyond the cliff, as if God were emptying his bladder.

The smell of wildflowers pierced my nostrils. The leaves trembled in the wind. I felt the humming of the earth. Slowly fog came from everywhere, gathering around our faces and covering our bodies like a blanket.

The color of the night began to sink into our skin. The moon cast its glow on a cloud. "Will there be wolves out tonight?" I asked, although I knew that wolves had disappeared from these parts a hundred years ago.

"Are you afraid?" Lion Head asked. His voice was filled with excitement. "I love darkness." He turned to look at me. His lion hair stood on its roots.

Lion Head asked me if I thought he was an attractive man. I told him that actually I used to think he was unattractive. He asked why. I reluctantly recalled that his shortness, his rawness, his arrogance had bothered me. He laughed. "What was it that made you change your mind?"

I admitted that Katherine's point of view had changed me.

She made me question my aesthetics and turned the beast into a beauty. Katherine taught me to respect nature as a whole, to appreciate individuality, to value uniqueness. It was in seeing him through Katherine's eyes that he became attractive to me, and it was because of my belief in Katherine that I began to be aware of beauty I had never thought existed. Lion Head nodded appreciatively and said that I was lucky.

I asked Lion Head about the way he grew up and about his family. He said that he was the eldest of seven children. His father was a dockworker and his mother a washwoman. She charged two cents per garment. From the time he was five years old, he collected and delivered clothes around town. Hunger was the prominent memory of his childhood. He said he did anything for food. He fed his brothers and sisters with the food he stole. He learned how to con people and once in a while he'd get caught and play innocent. He always got away. He became a self-educated opportunist at a very young age.

He was small for his age and had to fight his way through school. But his three-generation-true-proletarian background made him look politically reliable. He joined the Communist Party at sixteen and was honored as a good comrade every year.

He knew he was not what he seemed. While in school he stole books. Western books which made him realize what he truly desired. He managed to gain the trust of his Party bosses and peers. He made everyone believe he was sincere, that he would die for the Party. He made himself a humble man in the Party's eyes and he won privilege.

When he swore his allegiance at the Party's enrollment ceremony, he did not feel guilty about his lies. He firmly believed that to lie was the only way to live a truthful life.

Lion Head said he was honest with me because we were of the same kind. "You are a woman with a split personality," he said. "You are a masked lady during the day, just like I am a masked good guy. But we become our true selves at night. In the dark we can do things our way. When Chairman Mao closes his eyes, we come out to catch field rats like owls. We are too smart to starve, and too curious to waste our lives. The only way to be ourselves is to answer each other's call. Like radio waves in the air, we connect ourselves to the right channels."

I felt a chill and could not reply.

"Here we are, and this is our fate. I don't think you would sell me out, because we're on the same chopping block. We need each other, we are each other's spiritual food. Selling me out means selling out yourself. I know that you think this is cold and dispassionate, but let me tell you, I am passionate enough to come here with you, and you know the risk involved. Comfort me now and I will comfort you. Let's strip the great proletarian mask. Let's be naked, be bad, be animals. We'll be our hidden selves."

Lion Head took off his clothes. He lay down next to me. Tenderly he touched me. The warmth of his body stirred my insides. He began whispering. He said that he wondered if I understood the phrase "the spine of the wind," because that was what Lion Head was all about. He was the wind, he walked at the wind's will. His free-spirited soul was everywhere and nowhere. He came without a sound, went without a shadow.

Lion Head asked me to tell him where I came from. He wanted me to tell the story straight and flat, and I did. My family was from the southern part of the country. My grandfather worked as a bank clerk. He was a little man with a pair of thick glasses. He was scared all the time. He lost his job when his company went bankrupt. The family fled from the Shantung Province to Shanghai.

On their way to Shanghai my mother, a thirteen-year-old girl, had a nervous breakdown on the ship. There was an outbreak of typhoid fever on board. My mother's elder brother and younger sister were infected. There was no money, no doctor. The children were dying. The passengers were superstitious—they said that if anyone died on the ship, it would sink. Her dying brother and sister were thrown into the sea before they exhaled their last breath. My mother witnessed the scene in shock. No goodbyes, no tears. She broke down silently. Her family was no longer the same. A year later, in Shanghai, my grandmother died of throat cancer. My grandfather suffered sudden heart failure and died shortly after.

My mother married my father when she was a college student studying to become an elementary-school teacher. She believed that education was the only way to save China. My father was a grocery-shop clerk. I delivered goods for him from the time I was five.

Then came the Anti-rightist Movement. The Party security force arrested my father at midnight. I was sound asleep, dreaming about riding a train. There was noise. A group of people were knocking at our door violently. They broke in and took my father away. They said he was a capitalist promoter. The date was April 3, 1959; he and my mother had just celebrated their tenth wedding anniversary.

My father was charged as a traitor because he had worked as a policeman-in-training for the railroad before the 1949 Communist Liberation, when he was a middle-school student, a teenager. He was charged as a result of his confession. He could have hidden his past from the Party. He didn't have to tell the truth. He could have denied everything like so many of his colleagues. But he was an honest man.

My father thought serving as a policeman was not wrong. His intention was to protect passengers on trains who were working-class people.

Being honest killed my father. He was sentenced to twenty years in jail because one more body was needed to fill a quota established as a response to Chairman Mao's anti-rightist call. For twenty years my father left his wife and young children behind. I began to hate trains because they took my father away.

I was never the same after my father left. My mother's fairy tales lost their effect. The lesson I learned from my father was chiseled into my little brain. I learned that to be honest was to be stupid. I couldn't forget the moment my father was taken away. I could never trust again. My father was allowed to visit his family only once, when I was eight. Our life was ruined because of his sin.

My father was pronounced innocent in 1979. Two days before New Year's Eve he was released, with a piece of paper issued by the government saying he was a "good comrade." We went to pick him up at the train station. I didn't recognize him. I saw my mother take a blue cotton bag from an old man. The man walked with trembling legs. Mother told us to call him Dad. We did it awkwardly. My father's hair and beard were white. He said that he couldn't see very well. He almost got hit by a bus when we crossed the street. He sighed and sighed and rubbed his eyes all the time. He had strange habits. He had to sleep with the light on.

My mother had become an eccentric old lady. From the start she had a hard time with my father. She'd grown used to living all by herself. There were other men who had been nice to her. But for us, she waited for our father. She had dreamt about the family's reunion for the last twenty years. Now she had it. But my father was no longer the man she had known. Her expectations crashed.

My father turned into a lunatic. My mother would talk about her lost youth. She spoke about her bad luck for ever having married such a man. My mother made me sick to my bones with her complaining, but I could see her point. I couldn't stand my father either. His mind was still imprisoned. He was frightened all the time. He kept the windows shut all summer. He was afraid of the sunshine. He would rather sit and steam than come outside and enjoy the cool air. He would shout in his dreams, "Yes sir, death to reactionaries! Long live Chairman Mao!" Once he woke up the whole neighborhood. My mother said that he had been sent back from hell because he woke up the dead and the god of hell thought he was too much trouble.

I grew up on the street. I thought I deserved it because I had a father in jail. He was an enemy of the proletariat. I publicly denounced my father at ten. I took my mother's last name. I had the wildest imagination about the life I should have lived, a life free of guilt. I would make believe I was a revolutionary martyr's orphan. I would pretend I'd been injured in a car accident while saving the lives of three children and was brought to meet Chairman Mao. This is what I dreamt of throughout elementary school.

Lion Head was holding me, listening to me in the dark.

I didn't tell him much about Elephant Fields. I only told him that the village chief invited me to his family dinner the day I arrived. The family cooked a big bowl of rice for the occasion. I was waiting for the black lid to be lifted off when I realized it was a layer of flies. They formed a thick, dark fly-lid. I threw up.

Peasant families ate with the flies without a blink of the eye. I lived with one family for eight years, until I could eat with the flies without a blink of the eye, until my hair turned gray. I was twenty-six when I left.

Lion Head felt me shiver. He said I didn't have to go on. He said he understood that I lost all I had at Elephant Fields—youth, dreams, and most of all, faith. He said what I told was not just my story, it was the story of many of our generation.

I looked at Lion Head as he leaned over to kiss me. He whispered that we'd had enough misery and now we must enjoy life. Softly his hand began to touch my body. I became tense. My body was longing for intimacy, but my brain was not in sync. I could feel my mind split in two: I wanted to throw myself into Lion Head's embrace, but I resisted this journey of passion. I wanted to be loved, but I knew all I had with Lion Head was physical attraction.

He whispered that he was burning for me. His touches were oil on a fire. He murmured that he wanted me, and I heard my body moan in pleasure. My mind began to surrender. Sweat dripped from his forehead onto my face. I let myself be led.

The midnight wind began to whistle. The dog-tail grass brushed my face. I cried because it had been so long since I had allowed someone to touch me. Lion Head's gentleness made me believe I was loved. As he aroused my body, he aroused my memory.

Images presented themselves in full force without my mind's consent. Gray sky and dynamite, blood spreading down my legs, dyeing my shoes, wiping my bloody hand on the dry reeds, my running feet, the moving land, my voiceless scream, the horizon tilts . . .

Lion Head felt me shudder. He stopped. He hugged me tightly as if he knew. His fingers smoothed my cheek. I thought of Katherine, wished I were her so I wouldn't be so uneasy. The thought surprised me and made me think how much I had been wanting to be Katherine and not myself. I could hear Katherine's laughter, hear her sweet voice speaking Chinese.

Lion Head resumed his caresses. Until now I hadn't understood how much had been taken away from me. I put my arms around Lion Head. I felt like a child.

"You are a bird who's lost her wings," he said softly. "I want to give you new wings. I want to see you fly again. I want you to need me, to depend on me, to share the madness of desire with me. I'll throw the flashlight into the waterfall so we won't be able to go home, so we'll be scared. We will protect each other. We'll fight our fear together."

He rolled on top of me, touching me with his breath, massaging me with his words. "Don't worry. I will not enter you. Feel the wind's hand," he whispered in my ear. "Listen. I can hear the far sea moan. Listen carefully." My imagination rippled like the sea. "I can hear the wind sing in the trees." His hair swept my face and I heard him say, "Show me your wild summer, show me now."

He moved his body over me, then pulled away, away from my lips, my chest. "No," he said, clenching his teeth. "Don't break the rules. You'll be eaten by darkness, disfigured." Electric charges ran through my body. Our lust was like the chill of the grave. I wanted to beg him, beg him to touch me. I wanted to say, Please, please hold me. But I couldn't say it. I was ashamed of my desire. "Tell me you don't want this," he commanded. "Tell me you can live by yourself and be alone forever." I felt my body opening for him.

"Tell me you need me, say it, let me hear it, say it to me," he groaned. His head was wet, his mouth sweet.

"I want you," I heard myself say.

He grabbed me and shook me. "You poisoned snake, you thick cloud, you pouring rain, you hungry tiger, bite me, take my life, give me yours, I'll give myself to you."

He guided my hands to explore his body. He took pleasure in resisting pleasure. He enjoyed the torture, the cruelty. He watched me turn into a wild animal.

Our bodies began to wrestle. He wouldn't let himself have me. When his breath came heavier, he pulled himself back and rolled off my body, leaving my head against his knees. "Say you want me," he ordered, touching himself with my hand.

"I want you," I repeated after him breathlessly.

Like the sea roaring at a night of thunder, Lion Head lay on his back and wailed, "Oh, my wild horse! My poisonous scorpion! My sweet lilac, my fat lotus . . ." His other hand pulled at the grass, his feet digging pits in the earth, as he arched his body, exposing himself to the mid-moon.

My body trembled in violent pleasure.

"Wait for me," he murmured. "I will come again."

"I could tell you guys had something going on." Katherine's frankness embarrassed me, though I was eager to have someone to confide in. Katherine insisted on knowing what we did, how I felt, and whether I was in love. I didn't know what to say.

She asked if Lion Head was a good lover. I said that I had no way to compare. Katherine demanded the details. She wanted to learn the Chinese way, she said.

I was secretly pleased to have her attention.

"Lion Head wanted to please me and he wanted to know if I was pleased," I began my reporting.

"Were you?" Katherine asked. Her eyes were bright.

I told Katherine that I was not clear about my feelings. I didn't feel pleased or unpleased. I recognized my lust and it embarrassed me. I remembered the desire and I was not sure about the rest.

"It's all right not to be so clear," Katherine comforted me. "Your Zen masters say that one's true state is 'unclassified.' It's not meant to be learned. You know, like how the hand can't grasp itself. Then again there's the old American saying, 'Relationships are like buying a pair of shoes; you've got to try them on to see if they fit.'"

I did not like her American saying. Her dirty frankness bothered me. "I am no shoes to be tried on."

"Forgive me," she said. "You have to remember that I'm just trying to be your friend."

I told her that in China we called prostitutes "worn-out shoes."

The leaves outside my window looked like paper cutouts. I couldn't sleep. The world around me seemed so senseless, yet I could not stop myself from trying to make sense out of it. Maybe that's what Lion Head and I were to each other, an escape from the senseless world.

The way he talked about escape, though, was full of contradictions. He talked about letting the mind go and moving with the flow of change, like a ball in a mountain stream, how transcendence would be a kind of ecstasy, but then he would say: "I really want to go away. Far away and never come back. I want to go to a place where no one can abuse my will, where I'd be free to do whatever I pleased." He said he was just waiting for the chance. "Pray for me when you go to the temples," he said.

I tried to catch his thoughts but it was like trying to catch water with a sieve. When I asked him how he defined love, he sang me an ancient song.

> Chin-chin-tse-chin
> Youg-youg-wou-shin

> *The color of your scarf*
> *The spring of my heart*

> Chin-chin-tse-pei
> Youg-youg-wou-si

The lace of your jade
The thread of my craving

"Love is a song," Lion Head continued. "It's all in the presentation. I worship love for its magic and power. Do I know what it is? You're asking the wrong person. We grew up with hatred—how are we supposed to know love?"

That night I thought again of my father's life in jail. Of his solitary cell, no larger than a coffin, a small opening the only source of light and air. How it was impossible to stand up, how he lay on the bare concrete without a cot, how he was defenseless against the winter, how his joints were slowly destroyed. Twenty years of longing, every waking minute wondering how his wife and children were. Twenty years of severe loneliness. The Party believed "loneliness was the scalpel one used to perform surgery on the soul." My father relied on his imagination to survive.

Unlike Lion Head, I felt I knew love because I had experienced enough hatred. I knew what it was like to miss a dear person like my father as a child. I knew what it was like to sit on the corner, dreaming of greeting my father as he gets off the bus. I learned that the cruelty of winter teaches one to appreciate the warmth of spring—unbearable summer, the coolness of autumn.

I visited Katherine early one evening to look over her Chinese composition. It was an excuse to see her. She never mentioned paying me money again; perhaps she understood she could pay me back with her attention.

I found Katherine interesting no matter what she said or did. I collected in my mind the comments she dropped. She said amazing things that I had never thought of, like, "Give voice to your deepest and most immediate emotion." She would explain and explain until I understood what she meant. In this case she said she had been talking about the kind of emotion that existed in poems and that responded only to the thoughts and sensations that gave birth to poems.

Sometimes I could not follow her at all, but I would keep listening to her. I was in rapture, for she stimulated me in such an unfamiliar way. I watched her when she spoke. Sometimes I felt like I was dreaming. She was my window, and through its frame, I saw another world.

She laughed with such directness. When she learned that I was embarrassed about what happened with Lion Head at Wolf Teeth, she laughed. She kept saying to me, "Look, you are twenty-nine years old. If you were in America, you'd probably have been married and divorced by now. Big deal."

"No, no, no," I said. "You have missed my point . . ." I tried to explain. "You must understand the differences between East and West."

She said, "Oh, come on, underneath it all, people are the same."

She said that I was a nut, that Chinese were nuts in a lot of ways: "You're driving me crazy, and unfortunately I like it," she said, smoothing her hair with her hand. "You want to know something? I think you are wild. Just like me. Nobody can really tie you down. You know, you don't live with the foot-binding cloth anymore."

I looked at her. I nodded. I found her so beautiful. I wanted to be like her.

She laid out my thoughts for me. She was a sickle and I a

rake. I was amazed at her logic, the way she tallied her thoughts, pro and con, on a piece of paper with a pencil, how she made decisions. She said life was a process of making choices. One had to prepare for the inevitable deaths that came with change. She asked me to remember that there would be no choice that did not mean loss. She liked to sing, "You gotta win a little, lose a little . . ."

She made me learn from myself. She turned me into a sponge. I sucked the water of her knowledge. She told me that in America there were many psychotherapists, people who earned a living by discussing with people whatever was on their minds. "It's very expensive. Yet many Americans can't do without it. The more they pay, the better they feel. Some people believe the only way they'll be cured is if they pay too much."

Looking at my confused expression, she said: "Gee, you're so serious, you don't get my jokes at all, do you? That scares me, because I can't help kidding around. If you can't tell what's a joke and what's not, you'll be all messed up. Talk to me, don't give me that bull's face."

Katherine told me her secret wish was to adopt a child. I had a hard time comprehending her. I sat on her bed and looked at her. I had just finished telling her a story of a village family in my aunt's province who'd abandoned their baby just because it was a girl child. Katherine was in tears. "How could any parent possibly have the heart to do that?"

Katherine made me want to ignore her. She did not know that this type of story was not news to me. It happened in China too often.

Katherine refused to accept reality. I told her that she was drowning herself in other people's tragedy. She went silent. I saw her fury.

"You are cold," she said to me. "Cruel, you people." Her lynx eyes opened wide in anger, her pupils became big question marks.

I don't know how it happened, but at that moment, my heart felt a sudden tenderness. Her way of thinking touched me. It was something I had forgotten or maybe had never known. She unfolded the petals of my dry heart. A flower I did not know existed began to bloom inside me. It had been too long that my spirit had been paralyzed. I couldn't recall when I stopped feeling for my own people. Katherine stretched my life beyond its own circumstance. It was the kind of purity she preserved that moved me. She had a child's power. She pinned me to the wall and incited a revolution in my heart.

We sat by the window in her hut, facing the rice paddies. Watching farmers spread pig shit with their hands, listening to them curse the weather and the animals.

I told Katherine that I had always believed that circumstance made me who I was and I believed firmly that humans were born evil. I believed it was a universal truth because I lived through it. Survivors were people who took only what was useful for the moment and abandoned the rest. They refused to understand shame. Did the parents who abandoned their infant feel ashamed? They got rid of that baby just like they got rid of pus on their faces. They thought the pain was worth enduring. Hope was reborn when they laid the sleeping infant on the village road. They refused to hear her cries. They believed that when the sun rose everything would be forgotten. That was my China, not Katherine's.

I began to cry. Katherine was shocked at how emotional I'd become. She did not know what to do.

I told her that I did not appreciate her sentimentality. "You American, you lived a sugary life. What do you know about survival? Starving kids steal, cheat, and murder—they will do anything to fill their stomachs. This was my life. I gave up trying to reconcile with fate. It was not a baby I killed—it was me! Me!"

Katherine looked at me; slowly her eyes became gentle. She sat down beside me and took my hands in hers. She hugged me and I felt her tears on my cheek.

"I was seduced and raped," I began. I told her about my Party boss at Elephant Fields, Mr. Kee, a man of sixty. He tortured me when I started working there. He assigned me to the most danger-ous jobs. After a year he called me in and told me that he was removing me from the fields and making me his personal secre-tary. He took me to Party meetings and would touch me while we rode on tractors. He promised that he would send me back to Shanghai if I let him have his way with me. I was just twenty and far from home, but I didn't want to sell myself.

Mr. Kee sent me back to the fields to work with dynamite. I witnessed several fatal accidents on the job and I began to feel very scared. Mr. Kee invited me to a peasant's house during the Chinese New Year to "talk about my future." The peasant was a blind man. We sat on a big clay platform that was both the table and the bed. The house was lit with candles. I drank the wine Mr. Kee offered and I passed out shortly after. He had put drugs in the drink. Before I realized what was happening, I was raped. I could feel him undressing me, but I had no strength to move my limbs or make a sound. I lost consciousness. When I woke up,

Mr. Kee was gone and the blind man said that there had never been anyone but me in his house. I confronted Mr. Kee. He was eating dinner with his wife and family celebrating New Year's Eve. Wiping his oily mouth, he said he didn't know what I was talking about. He said that he had no such meeting with me. He accused me of insulting him and trying to ruin his reputation.

"Don't try to pull a hair from a tiger's head," he warned me.

I missed my period for two months. I couldn't stand the idea of being pregnant with Mr. Kee's beast inside me. I was too ashamed to go to a doctor. In China, any woman who got pregnant before marriage destroyed her future. I didn't know what to do about my growing belly. I ran, jumped, drank dirty water, worked overtime trying to get rid of it. But still I could not stop the little heart from beating. Mr. Kee saw what was happening and took me to see a relative of his who was a village witch. She made me drink Chinese medicine to poison the fetus.

The moment I drank down the medicine I realized that I would never be able to escape this fate. I was a mother who was murdering her child minute by minute. After work one day, I went to lie in the wild reeds. It was a cloudy and windy evening. I began talking to my dying baby. I asked for its forgiveness. I said I could not imagine what it felt like to have such a mother. I cried because it was too late, I had already taken the medicine. I tried not to think about which part of its body the poison had reached. I couldn't help but envision the process of deformation, I could see the medicine chewing up the heart, the limbs, the brain. I felt its struggle for life. I screamed up at God, asking why I was made to do this.

Three months old. Was it a girl or a boy? I felt part of me dying with it. I touched my swelling breasts. I thought she or he would never have my milk. The witch had told me about other women with unwanted children she had received. Most of them took her prescription and killed the fetus, but a few had delivered deformed babies. She gave me the address of an orphanage and told me to drop the baby secretly at night if I failed to abort it. Would the fetus die from the poison or come through me deformed? Every moment I wished for it to die. My mind was at the point of bursting.

Two weeks later, as I was pushing a cart filled with stones, I felt a warm stream gush out of my bottom parts. I ran toward the bushes. I could feel blood dripping down my legs. I hid myself in the bushes, I squatted down, and a bloody tissue dropped. It looked like a fish, a black-red fish. It was my half-formed baby.

I broke down. I couldn't touch it. I took off my blouse and tried to stop the blood from running. My hands were soaked in blood. I had no tears. My breath was short. I heard dynamite explode nearby as the world turned upside down. I fainted.

I woke up. It was early evening. I wanted to bury the "fish" but I had no strentgh. I laid reeds on top of it and ran away from it with all my might.

Katherine tightened her arms around my shoulders. She stroked my back tenderly. Holding her, I fell asleep in exhaustion.

Katherine stayed up all night.

I woke at dawn. Katherine was outside, sitting on a wooden stool, writing in her notebook. I walked toward her and she asked how I felt. I told her that every time I thought of Elephant Fields I despised life and hated the world.

Katherine gazed at me in the rising sunlight. "I don't know how to make you see life in another way. It's possible that we can never truly understand each other. But this is what I always say to myself in rough times: Life is not about giving up after a string of disappointments. Giving up is much easier than carrying on.

"Because my biological mother was blind and deaf, I used to think I might become blind and deaf at any moment. I still don't want to take the risk if there is even the slightest chance that a child of mine could turn out to be blind or deaf. But I don't allow myself to be bitter. I don't think life is unfair. We have this saying in America, it's actually a cliché: 'A pessimist sees a glass half-empty, an optimist sees it half-full.' It all depends on how you look at things. You see what I'm saying?"

I sat down next to Katherine. She handed me her notebook. I turned the pages. I couldn't read her flying handwriting. I turned to face her. She was in her brown sweater; her face was pale. She was looking at the sun.

Our two lives merged. I thought, Katherine who had every reason in the world to be cruel and cynical, who could have been a thief, a robber, a cheater, a drug user, a murderer, chose not to be. I saw how her spirit won out over fate. She woke me from my world of nightmares and brought me into the world of hope. She took away my bitterness, and a new mind began to take shape in me, a mind both wild and tame.

At the edge of the rice paddies, the sun jumped over the gray horizon like a giant fireball. I reached out for her. Without turning her head, she took my hands in hers. *"Tai-yang-nee-zao!"*— Good morning, Sunshine! she said, smiling, with tears glittering in her eyes.

Jasmine was furious. She made voodoo pictures with my name on them and burned them to ashes. It scared Lion Head, he told me one evening as we had tea at his grandmother's house. We were surrounded by antiques, a little ivory emperor and empress, fancy boats carved from redwood, copper horses, old embroidered draperies. Lion Head said that he hadn't slept well for days. Something was bothering him. He said, "I need to get my mind together." He tried not to tell me what was bothering him, but he could not keep his fears to himself. He finally admitted he was afraid of Mr. Han, Jasmine's father. And it killed our good time. We sat in silence, with Jasmine's curse upon us.

I decided to help Katherine adopt a child. I felt that it was a way to atone for my misdeed. I wrote all my relatives and asked them to help me contact orphanages and collect information.

Katherine spoke about her future child with determination. "I imagine her with single-lid slanting eyes, straight black hair, and a little cherry mouth. She will be standing behind a fence waiting for me."

My parents and my brother couldn't understand Katherine. "Why carry an extra load when one's own load is heavy enough?"

they asked. I couldn't explain to them what this meant, that it was way beyond carrying loads. No one in my family knew what happened to me at Elephant Fields. No one would understand that saving a child would help break the spell of bad memories that had been cast over me.

My father had me invite Katherine to the house for tea that Sunday. It surprised me that my father was not afraid of a foreigner. He treated Katherine like a daughter. When she stepped through the door, he pointed to a chair and said, "Sit," the way he would to me or my brother. He didn't say please. My mother was nervous and guarded the door to make sure no one was spying on us.

My father asked Katherine whether she was sure the adoption was what she wanted of her life, and whether she had considered the consequences if the child turned out to have birth defects in the future. Katherine told him that one could never really prepare for such things. She was indeed nervous, but determined to go forward.

My father turned to me. "I assume you understand your responsibility?" he asked. I nodded. "Be a wolf," he said, "when necessary." I nodded again.

"No, not a wolf," my mother protested. "How can you ask your child to act like a wolf? She should believe that morality wins in the end."

"I say be a wolf when you must!" my father said. Pointing a finger at Katherine, he continued, "Zebra will protect you. And I want your heart in one piece when it's done."

Katherine couldn't speak when she left my house. She said she would never forget my father.

On the way back from seeing Katherine off, I thought about

my father. I knew he adored me, but he never showed his feelings. He was sent to jail when I still a child. We never had the chance to be close, so we no longer tried. But today he showed me his love by treating Katherine as his own daughter.

Lion Head told me that he went to see Jasmine and spoke vicious words to her. He called her a "mad witch." He told her to stay out of his life. I asked how Jasmine reacted. Lion Head said that she was in a state of terror because he made her destroy the voodoo pictures.

But Jasmine didn't give up. Her eyes still said, "I love you, Lion Head," in every class. She stared at him, as if to say, I'll keep praying. I'll go on loving you until I die. She couldn't help it. She accepted the humiliation. She took it on as if it were her fate.

Though Lion Head walked out with coldness, he felt guilty. He believed that no one would ever love him as deeply as Jasmine. But he could not love her back. "I just can't touch her body," he'd say to me. Then: "She'll die for me, she will."

"What exactly did you tell her?" I asked.

"I told her that I loved differently," he replied. After a moment he sighed. "What else could I say? 'Go smell your farts, you bitch'? She would report me to her father and he would strangle my future."

Katherine asked me if Lion Head loved me. We were walking from school to her hut. Bicycles and buses passed us by, their bells ringing and horns blowing, but I couldn't hear a thing. The world around us did not exist. I told her that Lion Head said he loved me, but it was only words.

"Do you believe his words?" Katherine asked. I said that I had been trying to figure that out, but it was not the most important thing to me. What was important was why I was with Lion Head instead of anyone else. I asked Katherine if she thought there was a true definition of love.

"Don't ask me," she replied. "I wish I knew. I'm not as experienced as you seem to think." She told me she'd had many boyfriends, especially in Chinese terms. She'd had sweet times. "In America everything is easy, to the point of being boring. It's actually disgusting. Are you with me?"

I shook my head. I couldn't imagine easy things could be disgusting.

"Okay. Let's say I'm lonely. I meet a relatively attractive man at school or at a party, I enjoy his company, I flirt with him. No Party boss is looking over our shoulders, right? He comes on to me, and I encourage him. Maybe we go to the movies, have a nice dinner afterward, some nice wine, and things get looser. He offers to take me home. Tells me he thinks I'm beautiful and . . . Bam! There you have it. Could anything be more boring?

"I don't consider myself particularly lucky on the subject," she added. "Americans really have a surplus of everything except capital *P* for passion and capital *L* for love. Maybe I'm wrong. But beer and wine do not magical love make! After those kinds of encounters you inevitably feel lonely again, even if the person is still there. Oh God, I think about all the time I wasted. Move on, always tell yourself to move on."

I listened closely, immersing myself in her words.

"I did everything I could to 'find myself.' Like they say: sex, drugs, and rock and roll. And maybe some politics thrown in for good measure. My generation." Katherine sang these last words and laughed. "I can't even remember some of the things I've done. You can't outlive your generation, can you? Could you say no to Mao?"

"Of course not. I was part of Mao's growing tree," I said.

"Look, America is a free country, so free it's empty, nothing matters. No standards, no rules. I came to China because I had this fantasy. I thought China would be different. With its long history the people must be better rooted. I used to believe that Chinese people lived their philosophy, they sought the true meaning of life. Taoism, Zen, Buddhism all made great sense to me. But look at you, you're as confused as I am."

I was speechless. Katherine had a fantasy about China, I had one of America. Maybe the truth was there was no such "safe place" at all. Maybe we could only find this place, or create it, in our own hearts.

Katherine said that many times there was a voice screaming inside her that made her want to wipe herself out of this life. I said that it was true for me too.

We talked like this till late at night. She walked me back to school to get my bicycle. After I said goodbye to her, I felt a great hunger.

I went to visit Katherine nearly every night. We would sit around, sipping green tea. I taught her how to chew roasted melon seeds, how to use her tongue to split the seed in half, take in the sap, spit out the shell.

"This is how the villagers chew their nights away," I said.

"I like this," she said, concentrating on the act of chewing. "It feels like a kind of meditation."

"Are you really from the other side of the world?" I asked her.

"Oh, stop it," she said. "Would you just let me chew in peace?"

Once in a while, she would put on her lipstick while we talked. She'd take a rosy pencil, outline her lips, then fill in the lips with lipstick. She would keep talking, pressing her lips together to even out the color. To me it was terribly enjoyable.

She decorated her hut Chinese-style, using paper lamps, ink paintings, and old silk draperies she bought from the villagers. The villagers were curious at first. When Katherine was not around, they would come to peek through her lacy curtains. Soon they lost interest because Katherine was not as modern as they had expected.

I would try to get Katherine to tell me about men. I would say, "Tell me about the Latin boyfriend you had. Or the African boyfriend. Tell me again and again."

"What do you mean 'Latin boyfriend,' 'African boyfriend'? They weren't really *boyfriends!*" she would protest in embarrassment.

"It doesn't matter," I would say. "Just tell me everything I don't know, or tell me what I like to hear. Make up a story, I wouldn't know the difference anyway."

"You're terrible," Katherine would say.

But this is how I picture you in America, Katherine, I would want to say. Because I think you are so gorgeous, in my head I like to envision you laying your fabulous body next to a man.

When I lay on my bed, I realized what I had been missing in my life. For twenty-nine years I had been "in love" with Communism. I served my God, Chairman Mao. Now I was in love with the idea of getting to know Katherine, through whom I wished to relive my life. She taught me that freedom lay in our fighting arms, to be free was to be able to love someone enough to forget about yourself for even one moment. Through Katherine I began groping out of the tunnels of my life toward the rays of the sun.

"People usually end up telling on themselves," Katherine said one night at her hut. I was putting a washed mosquito net back on its bamboo-stick supports. She was looking through her notes from the interviews.

"I'm not sure if your 'common knowledge' applies here," I said, "because in China, people play everybody else's role but their own. I don't think you have a clue about what makes a Chinese."

"What do you think of your people?" Katherine stopped turning pages.

"I think I don't like them." I got off the bed. "I think I don't like Chinese people, because I don't like myself."

Katherine looked at me. She looked serious and sad.

"Well," I said, "maybe I am changing. Thanks to you." I went to sit next to her on the wooden bench. Katherine said nothing. Slowly, she bent over and kissed my cheek.

Lion Head was extremely interested in my conversations with Katherine. His eyes would brighten every time I gave him a report. He said everything about America interested him. He decided that the place he wanted to escape to was America. He was just waiting for the chance. He asked me to keep this a secret. He said if the school authorities ever found out, he would lose everything he had worked for. He said he loved me because he could trust me. He asked me to ask Katherine if he could join us in our private conversations, to learn more about America. Although I didn't want to have to share my intimacy with Katherine, I passed on Lion Head's message. A week later Katherine invited him to her thirty-seventh birthday party, along with fifteen of her other students.

For her birthday party Katherine planned a mountain-climbing trip on Sunday. She had gotten some information from a villager and learned that there was a famous platformlike place surrounded by the mists called the Shoulder of Beauty Tang. It was located midway up the Heavenly Peace Mountain, a four-hour train ride from Shanghai. Katherine bought train tickets for all fifteen of us in exchange for information. She wanted to learn the story of Beauty Tang.

We decided to meet on the mountain platform by two o'clock in the afternoon. So excited, I steamed three pots of bread and packed two jars of sweet-and-sour cabbage to take along. I took a bus to the train and approached the mountain on foot.

I read *Selected Readings from Ancient China* on the train. I discovered that Beauty Tang was a dancer, poet, and concubine of Prince Bian of the Han Dynasty, around 220 A.D.

After the death of the emperor, Prince Bian, who was eighteen years old, was brought forth to be the new emperor. There was a coup d'état, and General Tung Chou took the palace by force and held Prince Bian prisoner, forcing him to step down. The general staged a farewell party during which he intended to murder the prince by offering him a bronze bowl of poisoned wine.

Prince Bian knew death was approaching as he took the bowl.

Before he toasted the new ruler, he asked that his favorite concubine, Beauty Tang, be allowed to recite a poem together with him and dance for him:

> Prince Bian:
> *The road to heaven at this moment seems so difficult,*
> *I must give up your warmth and embrace loneliness.*
> *The nest is destroyed,*
> *Will any egg be unbroken?*
> *Leaving you, I will have no spirit.*

> Beauty Tang:
> *Without the sun there will forever be darkness.*
> *The collapse of your empire makes me no longer a concubine.*
> *Will there be any life after you have gone?*
> *Dance with me and let me be yours for the last time.*

It was said that Beauty Tang then showed her shoulder in the daylight for the first and last time. She knifed herself in honor of Prince Bian as she danced.

The trees were getting bigger and thicker. The leaves brushed my clothes and left strong minty smells. As I climbed, I thought of how Beauty Tang's story was so like the lives of Chinese women. Since ancient times we have lived lives of no choice. The only choice was self-sacrifice—in Beauty Tang's case, she killed herself at passion's highest moment, whereas I placed my soul in a cage.

Recently I had been ordered by my boss at the factory to withdraw from some classes and to become even more of a part-time student. As always, there was no explanation. "The assembly line needs more workers" was the automatic reason given. I had to work afternoons, and some night shifts, which meant that I would not be able to see Katherine as often.

As much as I resented it, I had no choice but to obey the Party's decision. I knew I would have to go back to my routine life once Katherine finished her teaching and left for America. She never told me how long she was allowed to stay in this country. I dared not ask her. I always had trouble accepting my fate. I tried to prepare myself for having nothing to do with her once she was gone. I just didn't want to spend the rest of my life working on an assembly line. I was asking for more than Chinese life could offer.

I felt stifled and Katherine was my oxygen. She would let go of China, but could I ever let go of America? Katherine's creation, America—was it just the product of a lonely Chinese's imagination?

Would my secret affair with Lion Head save me, I wondered. That he was not my type was the only thing I knew for sure. I had no expectations, but the act of rebellion stimulated me. It was his body, his lion hair, his flesh I touched, but it was my fear I was trying to conquer.

My youth was waving its hand in farewell but I wanted no more pity for myself. Taming my wild heart was the challenge I sought. Still, I was disgusted when I slept with Lion Head, with him and myself, always afterward, when we got up from his bed. I was ashamed of my lust. I could never look at him. I asked him not to look at me. But he always would when I asked him not to. He would look at me with strange eyes. Maybe he didn't know what to say or do, like me. He would tell me to sleep a while longer and close the door apologetically, leaving me to put on my clothes as he left without a goodbye.

Lion Head and I were obsessed with each other because of our fear of emptiness. I felt like I hardly knew him. I didn't care enough to know. Or maybe I was afraid of knowing because deep down I knew that we were together for the wrong reasons.

I went to his little room every other day to satisfy my flesh. We did not talk much. I told him I was sick of hearing Chinese philosophy, and he stopped talking. We let our bodies talk instead. Lion Head was in love with himself. It was obvious. He was not with me at Wolf Teeth. He watched himself when he lay on top of me. He made love to himself. Was I any better? One pair of cold hearts, two sides of ice. We shared the same hopelessness, the same faithlessness. Loneliness made us afraid of being alone.

The mountain air became fresher and lighter. I kept climbing. The sign said that I had arrived at the Shoulder of Beauty Tang, yet I saw no "shoulder." I couldn't figure out which part my feet were standing on—Beauty's neck, shoulder, or bosom? The near peaks looked like green dolphins shooting toward the sky from the ocean of mountains. I found a giant smooth stone under a pine tree. I lay down on the cool stone and felt peace. It was almost two. The sky was low—one moment it filled with thick clouds; the next, the sun broke through. There was no one else around. I breathed the air, dreaming about how Beauty Tang moved as she danced before her lover. At least she knew that the last thought the prince would have before he kissed death was of her. Wasn't that all an ancient concubine hoped for?

I closed my eyes. I could feel my thoughts calm down, slowly swimming between the veins of my brain. Time stopped. The Han Dynasty drum music faded from my head. I could hear my own sizzling thoughts crawling toward the shore of the brain's river. I heard a sudden laugh break through the quietness. It was familiar. I heard it again. I was not daydreaming. I opened my eyes.

Across a deep valley, over on the opposite peak, about one hundred yards away, Lion Head and Katherine hung from a vine of ivy, lowering themselves toward a narrow rocky ledge. Lion Head was in control. He held Katherine on his lap, locking his arms around her waist. Bit by bit they swayed down.

I got up and hid myself behind a pine tree.

The valley was deep. They would fall if they were not careful. The mountain echoed with Katherine's laughter and screams.

I was surprised but not shocked. I knew there was an attraction between Katherine and Lion Head. I had admitted to her that I didn't love Lion Head and maybe I even encouraged her to seduce him. I didn't know why, but I always pictured the two of them together. I liked discussing Katherine with Lion Head. I once asked him to imagine how Katherine would moan when she made love. We both had fantasies about it. My desire to learn how Katherine made love to a man was stronger than my desire for Lion Head.

Was Lion Head different from her other men? He was showing her risk, adventure, filling her ear with Chinese philosophy, Lion Head–style. A vinegar jar broke inside me, bitter and sour.

Lion Head was taking his time with Katherine. His body was glued to hers. I did know him well. He enjoyed the "sweet torture." He wanted her to feel his maleness, his determination, his heavy breath. I imagined her eyes closed, doing what he instructed. Was she trying to resist him? He would play with her by telling her to let go. He would tell her what ancient Chinese lovers did on ivy swings, rubbing and teasing their bodies. He would flood her with his storming knowledge of history. He would tell her that the process of rebirth was from moment to moment. He would explain his theory of the impermanence of the world and tell her to resist the effort of trying to grasp things. He would suggest she listen to her body, and she would, and then he would make her his . . .

I felt admiration for Lion Head as much as jealousy. I remembered the way he seduced me. He did not have to touch me to get me excited. He was doing the same thing to this American woman. I was curious about her reaction to his touch, the touch of a Chinese man. My jealousy became insignificant for the moment. If this was a betrayal, I deserved it because I was never sincere with Lion Head. I now realized how little I cared about him. My thoughts went to Katherine. I knew she couldn't love Lion Head. She told me more than once the image she had of Chinese men when she was growing up, how even the idea of being with a Chinese man seemed ridiculous. She told me that in America, Chinese men looked to her like "funny-looking little eunuchs." In a way, I wanted Lion Head to show her a Chinese man's muscle. I wanted to have him torture Katherine, mistreat her, beat the eunuch idea out of her head. I knew Lion Head would be good for the job, I knew he could make her beg.

I smelled the needles of the pine tree. Katherine once said that in America people feared passion, they laughed at those who loved too much. And still people longed to feel. What was she feeling now? Animal passion? Did the Chinese landscape make her bolder and her desire stronger? I felt her shivering and excitement.

They lowered themselves onto the small stone ledge. The space barely fit two. I saw Lion Head begin to unbutton Katherine's shirt.

Clouds began to obscure the sun, and the color of the mountain darkened. I felt a raindrop fall on my hot face. I rubbed my eyes, held my breath. Lion Head buried his face in Katherine's bosom. Gradually she stopped pushing him away. He started to explore her. Her invitation was silent. I could hear Lion Head groan. Katherine dared not move too much. If she did, they would fall into the valley.

He kissed her madly. He locked her fingers in his hands. His arms were strong. She seemed drunk with pleasure and frightened at the same time. She arched her chest, exposing her breasts. She raised one of her legs, slowly, and wrapped it around his hip as he devoured her.

She kissed him back, then stopped. She pushed him away. He insisted. He bit to open her shirt. She gave in. She began stroking his hair with her fingers. She was mothering him. Her swanlike neck bent back, her face toward the sky, and he entered her.

I could feel Lion Head move inside me. I knew what Katherine was feeling. Her shiver of pleasure, her madness of wanting more. I entered Katherine through Lion Head. I could hear her moan, exactly as I had imagined.

He watched her, her swelling breasts, her milky skin and flaming eyes.

With the echo of Lion Head's groan, the mountain became enclosed in a white curtain of rain. The curtain grew thicker and finally blocked my sight.

The wildness disappeared from my mind's eye.

Before long the shower stopped. The sun came out and mocked the naughty rain. A rainbow began to form between the peaks. All of a sudden, I saw the outline of a shoulder-shaped peak in the sunshine—the Shoulder of Beauty Tang. It was a fresh green and the rainbow looked like a lacy sleeve. I envied the ancient woman because she had known a perfect passion.

Jasmine and I ran into each other on our way to the "shoulder." She was in a talkative mood. For the first time, I felt like talking to her a little. I hoped the conversation could stop my running thoughts. Jasmine portrayed herself as a victim of love. She wore a light yellow shirt and a matching knit skirt. She said that she kept getting eye infections because she couldn't help crying whenever she saw Lion Head. She said that she only ate six pieces of noodle a day and could hardly sleep. She was lovesick. She would die for him. She believed that she had already begun to die. I noticed that her flying eyebrows were now the shape of two dropping geese shot by gunfire. Her cheeks were streaked with the trail of tears.

"You can believe it or not, but I will die soon," she said. She spoke about death with such nobility in her voice. She said she wasn't complaining. "I shall never resent him. He can have his freedom once I am dead."

I had nothing to say. She didn't seem to need my comfort. She needed only an audience for her performance. She had secretly written a letter to Lion Head, she said. She hoped that he would find out about it and read it after her death. "He will realize what great love he missed, but by then it will be too late," she said. "Too late for him to cry over me."

Jasmine waited for me to offer to tell Lion Head about the letter waiting for him.

I looked at Jasmine; I was not going to fulfill her wish.

"Nobody dies from lovesickness," I said. "Not in our time. Not anymore."

Finally the birthday party took place in the mist. All fifteen of us arrived. Laying out food and drink, we began singing and playing traditional music with harmonicas. Jim brought a cassette player and played Katherine a piece of music by a friend of his who was an underground composer. The music was based on the Ming Dynasty play *The Peony Pavilion* by Tang Xian-zu, a playwright compared with Shakespeare, Jim explained. It was the story of a romance between a poor scholar and the daughter of a rich lord, and it had a happy ending. Katherine was greatly pleased. She sat apart from Lion Head, as if nothing had happened between them just an hour ago. Lion Head looked unusually serious.

Clouds sat above our heads. Wind brushed through the leaves. Although it was late autumn, the mountain held the noon heat. It felt like summer. Squirrels tried to get closer and steal our food.

Katherine did not know that she held power over our future. If she told the school authority that this or that one was a linguistically gifted student, then that person would have a great chance at an important post, such as being appointed a secretary in the Department of International Relations, or a clerk in the Bureau of Foreign Affairs. A post unlike one any of us now held. A dream.

The birthday party gave the students the chance to flatter their teacher. Katherine was showered with gifts we were not able to afford but bought anyway. We were in competition to please the foreign devil. Katherine knew nothing of what was on our minds. She trusted us too much. She would never think she was being used in such a way. The Chinese believed in the saying "One's sharp tongue becomes blunt when one takes the other's food; one's arm becomes shorter when one picks up the other's gift." The people in the class believed that gifts would buy them a good impression, which would turn into words of praise to be dropped in the Party's dossier. Yet my classmates liked to believe that they were not superficial, not opportunistic, that their gifts did not mean to buy Katherine's favor. They preferred to think of themselves as nice people, people with a great history of being kind and generous.

"We Chinese value great friendship. Long live our great friendship," everybody said as the gifts were unwrapped.

Katherine was like a happy schoolgirl. Lion Head gave her a silk robe embroidered with peonies. Jim gave her a set of long necklaces made of pieces of hairpins from his great-grandmother's opera costumes. Jasmine bought her a set of ancient minibattleships carved from ivory. I bought her a white-and-green-jade hand mirror and comb. Katherine got bamboo table mats, expensive slippers, crystal hand massagers, an ivory shower claw, a hand fan made of animal bones. We spent all we could to buy our good impressions.

Katherine looked at me twice as she took my gift. Was she wondering if I sensed that something had happened between her and Lion Head? I returned her look and smiled. She looked uneasy. She could tell I knew something. I left her to cook her doubts. I decided to wait until they boiled and spilled over the top.

Jim took out his Yangtze River—brand camera and wanted us to pose for pictures. The men looked for good backdrops while the women fixed themselves up. Jasmine took out a red hair band and pushed it back on her head. She looked like a big turkey. I took out a black jacket with a chrysanthemum pattern. I'd bought the jacket to match Katherine's taste in black.

Katherine opened her bag and took out a tube of reddish lipstick. She was in a tight brown cashmere sweater. She avoided my eyes. She sat quietly on a rock, brushing her face with powder. The mountain heat maintained its intensity. I suddenly remembered how Katherine had once told me that she loved summer for its heat.

She sat, motionless and elegant, as if trying to absorb the warmth of the air. Everyone watched her, trying not to stare, taking in the wide, thin back, the long arms, the round, horselike hips, and the bosoms that stuck out like tomatoes. She made the women self-conscious with just her presence. Each man, except Lion Head, asked to have his picture taken with the teacher. Jim the cameraman got to take two with her, one with his arm around her shoulder. The women wanted to eat her up.

We made toasts with Chinese wine that was soft in taste but strong. Katherine became more talkative. She said she had never gotten drunk on wine before, but then again she had never tried with Chinese wine, especially Green Bamboo. Jim told her Chinese wine was just like Chinese culture—it worked slowly but potently. One could get intoxicated without knowing. Katherine asked for more. Her Chinese began to knot, and she began to speak fast in English.

Everybody was getting more animated. Our tongues loosened. The men stared at Katherine's body freely.

Katherine asked about the assignment on the Shoulder of Beauty Tang. Everyone reported the same story I learned. But I was the only one to come up with Beauty Tang's poem.

Katherine cracked her rose-colored lips as she listened to the story of Beauty Tang's passion. The men drew closer to her and sipped more wine. The women watched the men at first, but soon we too focused our eyes on her, watching Katherine's lips pronounce, "What a story! What a woman!"

We made no response. Beauty Tang was not on our minds. The Chinese classic had much less impact on us than the foreign devil's red lips.

Katherine became self-conscious. She changed her pose several times. Still uncomfortable, she said: "It's my lipstick, isn't it? What are you staring at? Is my lipstick bothering you? I can take it off." She took out her handkerchief.

Lion Head came up to her and froze her arm with his hand. "It's your birthday," he said, taking away her handkerchief and stuffing it in his jacket pocket. "Allow us to appreciate the beauty of nature."

Katherine looked up at Lion Head. She saw a pair of burning eyes. She opened her makeup bag. "I want to do a face," she said. "I want to do a Chinese face! Any volunteers?"

Jim stood up and we giggled. "How about me?"

Lion Head pushed him away. The men shoved him and punched Jim playfully. "A mouse offers to wipe the oily kitchen counter! What an opportunist. Get out of here!" they said.

I saw Jasmine's O-shaped mouth twist, as if she were about to make up her mind. I thought about Katherine's fingers touching my face, about smelling her perfume, about how she would make me look like her. I stood up and sat down in front of her right before Jasmine took action.

"Do my face, if you please," I said, staring into her eyes.

It took her forty-five minutes. She lit a cigarette before she began. She turned aside as she exhaled the smoke, but the wind blew it back in my direction. I smelled her breath, along with her fragrance.

She was patient. She applied the base with her fingertips. You westerners call yourselves civilized people, I thought, but you, Katherine, seem to be from the wild jungle of animal instinct. You've begun an affair with Lion Head. Do you like conquering our men? Without effort, you won our men's admiration. How does that make you feel?

Her brush moved here and there as she put on the eye shadow. China is easy for you, Katherine. I am sure soon you will find it boring. I can tell—I see it written on your face, etched into your wrinkles. You will find it all smells like spoiled dirty dishes.

I studied her features in detail as she rubbed my cheeks with rouge. The sculptural contours, the deep-set, double-lidded, almond-shaped eyes filled with unspeakable energy, the irises like ripples in the river. The tip of her nose was inches away from mine. It was a bony nose compared to flat Chinese meatball-like noses. What's marinating inside this head-jar? Do you know what you're taking away from me? You spoke of respect but you take pleasure in stealing Lion Head. You care only about satisfying your lust, just like me. Could it be that you are lonely too?

I examined the texture of her skin and the tiny veins underneath. Her warm breath kept hitting my face. I felt the tip of her pencil outlining my lips. Her long eyelashes blinked as if aware of my staring. Her cheeks suddenly turned red. What now? Have your hands told you what I am thinking?

The men said I looked like a westerner. They said a Chinese woman could never do that to herself. That was why all Chinese women looked like midwives, like the dregs of tofu. Now these men believed that their own women could look desirable too. It was just makeup, after all. Thank you, Katherine, for the enlightenment. I thought how Chinese men, creators of the foot-binding tradition, the tradition that was inspired by the sway of the willows, were now pronouncing a new aesthetic on how women should look. I should have been grateful for the lesson, but I was not. I wore Katherine's face and for a moment I could pretend to be American, but I was not Katherine. I could never be her. Even if I could be her, with this borrowed face, I would not.

We returned to the city and Katherine invited us back to her hut to dance. We were never this wild in our lives, except during the Cultural Revolution when we copied Mao's teachings on the walls. We worked through the night and sang, "We love you, our dearest Chairman / We're ready to open our chests and offer you our hearts."

Katherine lit three candles, and all of a sudden the room looked like the enemy's rooms depicted in our propaganda movies. We did not say this to Katherine. We didn't want to spoil her mood; we didn't want to make her cautious. Lion Head, Jim, and I spoke to each other without opening our mouths. We were trained to think alike with little different "personality flavor." We thought as one in silence. We carefully kept Katherine from knowing too much because once she learned the rules, she would become one of us, she would become Chinese and we would lose touch with the America she had created in our minds. We were old Chinese master painters, trained in the rules of tradition for so many years we'd lost the "heavenly joy" we were supposed to gain. We could never splash ink on rice paper to make a wild landscape the way a child would. Katherine was our child; we wanted her to draw from her imagination so we could rediscover innocence.

We pretended the room was brightly lit. We sat around Katherine as she began to move her body to the American music. We prepared our escape in case the authorities broke in. Everyone but Katherine knew that dancing by candlelight was forbidden in China. Secretly we took turns watching for police outside the hut. Now it was Jim's turn. He stood in the dark, pretending to smoke. We could be arrested and thrown into detention houses. Someone like Jasmine might get away with it because of her father, but not the rest of us. Yet no one wanted to leave. It was too exciting to be missed.

Katherine twisted her hips as she danced. To us, dance meant striking Mao's propaganda poses. We threw up our hands, made a motion of opening hearts, and sang, "Chairman Mao, and the Great Party, we love you with all our hearts and souls." We made kicking poses, stabbing poses, we shouted, "Down with bourgeois imperialism!" We didn't know there was another way to dance until recently. We'd heard about it because of the country's new "open door" policy, but we'd never seen it with our own eyes. Katherine's dance was so animal-like. She reminded me of a writhing snake, a swimming sea lion, a chewing silkworm, a chopping woodpecker.

This is corruption, my mind said. If you don't want to resist, at least you should not actively participate. But the foreign devil was getting under my skin. It was hard to sit still. I watched Katherine swing her body and my bones began to itch.

Katherine asked Jim to stand up, relax, and move his body in sync with hers. She called this the "spoon dance." She pasted her body onto his and rocked slowly. She didn't know what she was doing to our heads. We were defenseless against this bourgeois influence.

I did not know that I was so ready to embrace the devil, though I needed little persuasion. I fell into a trap I had set for myself. I was there, ready; she only had to show me the way and I went.

Who was not their true self that night? Who did not break the authority's rules? Who did not enjoy the sensation? Jasmine sat on a bench, rocking on her buttocks. She was nearly drooling. No one would ever admit to any of this. Not even to themselves. This was how we were raised. To be unconscious of one's feet implies that the shoes are too comfortable, our ancestors taught us. To be unconscious of one's waist implies that the girdle is too loose. It was in our tradition to have two minds. We learned to say one thing and do another. We trained ourselves to become like Chui, the ancient artisan who could draw circles with his hand better than with a compass. His fingers accommodated themselves naturally to his subject, so that it was unnecessary for him to focus his attention on it.

We appeared humble and submissive. We shut the eyes of the heart to make peace with tradition. We could say the Cultural

Revolution never happened. We hadn't meant it when we shouted "Long live Chairman Mao!" We could say we were young, only children, we can't really remember. We followed the example of the government and said that we wanted to turn our eyes to the future.

We were studying English in order to fight with imperialists. If anyone asked us what we did tonight, we would say we did nothing with the foreign devil.

Katherine spooned my body and swayed slowly. She held me as we danced, her hands on my thighs. I smiled like a drunkard. She moved me with the rhythm of the music. Her hands were on my shoulders, my waist, my hips. She laughed and said, "Your body moves like a stiff windmill."

Her bracelet, her necklace. I breathed in her scent. The music, the joy, her rosy lipstick. I thought of the Beatles song because she was holding my hands and I let her. Her body brushed against mine again and again. Before the eyes of everyone in the room. I held my breath. We were in America.

My parents were sound asleep like the billion others in this country. In their confusion, they gave up on me, their daughter of no piety.

My brother was talking in his sleep. He sounded like a gold-fish making air bubbles in the water.

I rose at dawn. In the dark I heard the sound of rain like beans jumping in a hot wok. I thought I would read to put myself back to sleep.

Switching on my dim bedside light, I took a book out from under my pillow, *Ancient Poems of the Middle Kingdom.* I was up to the nineteenth century, at a poem by a poet with an ancient name spelled with a character I could not even pronounce. It was called "The Love of the Immortals." I read and my mind became wildly awake.

> On your slender body
> Your jade and coral girdle ornaments chime
> Like those of a celestial companion
> Come from the Green Jade City of Heaven.
> One smile from you when we meet,
> And I become speechless and forget every word.
> For too long you have gathered flowers
> And leaned against the bamboo,
> Your green sleeves growing cold
> In your deserted valley:
> I can visualize you all alone,
> A girl harboring her cryptic thoughts.
> You glow like a perfumed lamp
> In the gathering shadows.
> We play wine games
> And recite each other's poems.
> Then you sing "Remembering South of the River,"
> We paint each other's beautiful eyebrows.
> I want to possess you completely—
> Your jade body
> And your promised heart.
> It is spring.
> Vast mists cover the Five Lakes.
> My dear, let me buy a red-painted boat
> And carry you away.

I could not articulate even dimly within my mind what I was feeling. I began to feel as if I were being taken, carried away, and reeled back by a force I could only sense. I was being transformed. Katherine, the foreign devil, in her hands, I was reinvented. Everything I saw, I saw now with eyes made by her. The poem which I had read before was no longer the same poem. The love of the immortals, the red-painted boat.

If she were a building, he was determined to demolish it. At first Lion Head seemed not to care how Katherine treated him; then, when he understood that there was no way he could possess her, he lost his mind. The frustrated lion showed his claws. From that moment on, in her eyes, his beauty began to fade. She became the naughty mouse to his blind cat. She let him chase her. She toyed with him, driving him mad, and then escaped up a tree. Then she turned into something else, and when the cat in confusion looked up the tree, he saw no mouse, only a bird that laughed and shit on his face.

Katherine spoke with Lion Head after school. She asked him to "get serious" with his homework, or she would have to fail him. We were making great progress with our English. We were able to read Hemingway and Brontë. Lion Head was no longer too good for the class. "I have the whole class watching me," Katherine warned him. "I can't grant you special favors. It'd be unfair to the others."

The winter of 1983 was bitter for Lion Head. He fell in love with the foreign devil and was spellbound. He received no comfort from me. He deserved this because he betrayed me.

I didn't invite Katherine home for the New Year holiday

although my parents insisted, especially my father. "Aren't you good friends?" asked my father. I didn't tell my father that I wanted to punish Katherine for stealing Lion Head.

Katherine must have spent her holiday all alone, since she had nowhere to go. It was the first Christmas she spent without her family in America. She thought she would have many places to go and many families to visit. I knew she had counted on me. I felt bad about punishing her, but that was the only way I would forgive her.

I missed Katherine every day during the holiday. Even the neighborhood fireworks—my favorite part of New Year's Eve—didn't excite me. I imagined Katherine alone in her hut. I held myself back and tried hard not to write her. A few times I had such an urge to get on a bus and throw myself at her door. I found myself waiting anxiously for the spring term to begin.

Early one morning I was on my way to the market, carrying a bamboo basket. I saw two little girls, about two or three years old, walking in front of me, hand in hand. They stopped and clumsily one girl tried to button up the other's coat. How beautiful! I thought, and immediately I was amazed. I was rediscovering my long-lost sensitivity. My heart was becoming tender again. My mind went to Katherine, who taught me to love again like a child.

I wrote Katherine a letter telling her about this experience. But I tore it up in front of the post office. "A snake should never attempt to get a taste of heaven: once seduced it will never be able to go back to hell where it belongs." I was afraid. If I ran to Katherine, she would take away my heart and leave my body an empty shell.

The spring term began. I got up early and washed with soap-tree fruit so I would smell good. I put on a navy blue Mao jacket and pants and People's Liberation Army boots, an outfit no Chinese would wear anymore. I arrived too soon and bicycled around the campus. There were many new faces, young and fresh-looking.

I checked the bulletin board. My heart tightened as my eyes moved over the class listings. My sight blurred in nervousness. I was to report to a new classroom, but Katherine was still our class's main instructor. When her name, the Chinese character for "peony," came into focus, I let go a long breath. My steps carried me quickly to the door of the new room.

She had a new haircut. The jellyfish-tail hair that spread down her back was gone. She was in a beige sweater, black jeans, and a silver belt. She stood before the blackboard, looking out the window, her back to the door, as if deep in thought. She was alone in the room.

I stood as if frozen. The wind blew open the door. She turned and saw me. A little awkwardly, she smiled.

I made myself say hi.

"You look wonderful," she said, like her old self. "I like your outfit a lot."

I dressed up for you, I thought.

She looked at me as if studying my face.

I felt her fingertips running across my cheeks.

My classmates began to arrive. She was taken away. She glanced at me as she said hello to them.

I took a corner seat.

Lion Head showed up quietly. Jasmine followed, carrying his green army bag. Lion Head was in a high-collared brown cotton winter coat. He sat by himself in a seat off to the side without saying hello to anyone. Jasmine passed his bag to him and hesitated for a moment before finally sitting down one seat behind him.

Katherine got up in front of the lecture table. Her smile was just as beautiful as last year's. "I got a lot done during the New Year break," she began. "I was more alone than I'd ever been in my whole *ta-ma-de* American life." A few giggled at her use of swear words. She looked at me. "But it was good. A good experience, a Chinese experience, for sure." She began pacing. "I answered letters, worked on my dissertation, and finally finished reading *Dream of the Red Chamber*." She turned away from me. "It made a lot of sense to me. A lot of sense. I must thank you for such an education. Now let's begin our text on Virginia Woolf."

She will forgive me if she understood the essence of the book, the essence of the Chinese way, I thought, and felt a little relieved.

Katherine told the class that she was glad to learn that the Central Bureau's new policy sought to improve East-West communications, which meant she would have a little more freedom in choosing texts.

We showed her an expressionless face. To us this was not news. The Central Bureau could open the door at any time but that didn't mean it would stay open.

Lion Head watched Katherine, his face twisted, his hair standing up from the roots. In an effort to get away from Katherine, he traveled to the North over the holiday. But he came back still unable to find his mind. He had never been this way with me or, I believed, with any other woman. He had never been in love with anyone but himself. I saw a flame of anger in his eyes. He was a wounded bull.

He'd always been lucky with women. Like the petals of peach flowers, they rained down on him, just fell on his face, and all he had to do was smell the fragrance. When he was no longer interested, he would brush the petals off, stamp them into the mud, let them turn brown, dry, and blow away in the wind. Then he would sigh, "Oh, what a beautiful day!" and with a smile he would look toward the new spring.

But the winter storm of 1983 made its appearance without warning. The chill zipped through Lion Head and froze him. He did not know if his heart would survive the new year.

Katherine looked at him with remoteness. Are you all right? her eyes asked him. Mirrors of a clear lake, her eyes, so clear that on their crystal surface his thoughts were reflected. He was exposed, inside out. He had gotten himself drunk on gasoline, and with the spark from her eyes he set himself on this burning journey.

He could not bear her polite, concerned looks. I could tell he was having a hard time just being near her. At the break he asked if she wanted to see some new antiques he'd collected. She said, "Thanks, maybe some other time."

He said, "May I help you with your Chinese?"

She said, "That's okay, no thanks."

He said, "*He-bi-ne?*" Why are you giving me such a hard time?

She said, "I don't get what you're saying."

He said, "Please stop doing this to me."

She said, "What are you talking about?"

The class watched. And pitied Lion Head. After all, Lion

Head was a Chinese. We could not help but be on his side. Whether I loved Lion Head or not was another issue. We secretly wished that Katherine would suffer a little. We needed to see her suffer, to balance things out. Lion Head had never lost himself over one of us. In this, Jasmine and I were comrades.

Late Thursday afternoon I was making light switches. The molding machine had been on all day. It sounded like a helicopter. I had done four loads of switches since morning. I could not help feeling scared wondering what would happen after the term ended, where I would be, what I would be assigned to do. The factory boss who had been so interested in having me translate his product catalogue had been charged with corruption and transferred. He was caught using factory funds to entertain his relatives. I was once again a worker borrowed from Elephant Fields. I lost sleep at night. I set my sights on being the best student in the class; if a good opportunity arose, I would be the one best equipped to grasp it.

I spent even less time with my family. My brother finally got married and had taken over my room. His thirty-nine-year-old bride just couldn't wait any longer. I had to sleep with my parents. At night, when I came home, I wouldn't turn on a light so as not to wake my parents. I did everything in the dark: eat, wash, and change clothes. It made me angry. The anger was nameless. I conducted my life like a prisoner making his escape, waiting, as I ran, for the bullet to hit me in the head or maybe miss.

Lion Head came to the factory to look for me. He waved at me from the window, but I could not hear what he was saying.

I turned off the machine and took off my cotton gloves. I asked why he had come. He didn't answer my question but said that he had to talk to me and did not mind waiting. He went to sit in a corner and lit a cigarette.

I went up to him and said, "I have ten minutes."

He said that he needed more than ten minutes.

Lion Head and I went to a noodle shop after I got off work. He ordered two bowls of noodles with weed-hearts. I shoved the stuff down. The yellow-white weed-hearts were tender. I waited for Lion Head to speak.

"I'd like to get serious," he said. He wanted to have a relationship, a family, a future with me.

"This is stupid," I said in a sarcastic voice. "What about your foreign object?".

"She's a bitch," he said. "She seduced me. It was a good lesson. It made me understand how much I love *you*. I can't live without you."

I wanted to laugh but I managed not to insult him. Who was this man? I couldn't believe that I had once desired him so much. He was trying to use me to get back at Katherine.

"But you love her," I said, catching his eyes. "How can you deny that? You're fooling yourself."

"No, I never loved her. It was curiosity. I'll confess that I was after her meat. It's a weakness all men unfortunately possess. But . . . but I need to share a soul with someone, a Chinese soul."

Lion Head insisted on having tea with me that night. He said he was going through a tough time and needed company. He begged me to stay with him. About eight o'clock in the evening I went with him to his little room. He did not turn on the light. He locked the door, turned around, stood face-to-face with me for a moment, then he pulled me down, his arms around my shoulders, pushed me down on his bed, and threw himself on top of me. I thought, Oh, how awful. I lay there. I heard my stomach groan. He began to do the same things he did with me at Wolf Teeth. But there was no magic. My body was numb. Cold. I felt no blood running in my veins. He stopped, and after a while he began to sob. He said that God must be punishing him.

We sat up, in the dark, each facing the wall.

He began to talk about our past. How beautiful it all was. He talked about the time of the Cultural Revolution, the heroes and the glory, our culture a thick wall no foreigner could break through. Our straight black hair, our yellow-brown skin, the beauty of our race, our five-thousand-year-old history, the styles of calligraphy, the artistry of the brush stroke, the colors, the ink, Chineseness.

Katherine was honored as the year's teacher of merit by the school authorities. She was given a three-day vacation. She told me that she had contacted several orphanages and had one in mind to visit. She asked me whether I would like to accompany her. Immediately I said yes.

I went to get a permit to leave my job for three days. The unit head would not grant me permission unless someone was dying in the family.

I lied. I said that my grandmother was dying and she needed to see me to let go. The unit head made me promise that when I returned I would catch up on all the switches I left behind.

Katherine and I took separate routes. We took different buses in order to cover my lie. We snuck out of Shanghai without being seen together. She was very excited. She told me that it was like a James Bond movie. When I asked what that meant, she explained that it had something to do with being adventurous. She then asked how I felt about the adoption. I said that I didn't feel much; I felt normal. She shrugged her shoulders.

The Yi-lian train station was located in a northern suburb of the city. There was a big crowd. The locals wore dark brown clothes. We were squeezed into a big waiting room. The peasants sat on the concrete floor. Everyone had the same sagging expression, like prisoners waiting to be released.

I wore an old scarf on my head that covered half my face. Katherine said that she could hardly tell me apart from the locals. I told her that she didn't look too good either. She had on no makeup and was wearing a worn-out deep blue jacket with big buttons from her chin to her knees. A pair of black lantern pants tied at the ankles. Black cotton shoes with rubber soles. Her feet looked huge. She also had a bright red-and-green-flowered scarf wrapped around her head. She looked like a man in a scarf from behind. She stood like a horse among goats. One woman passenger called her *"Da-shu"*—Big Uncle—when she asked Katherine to make space so she and her baskets with two babies in each could get by. The woman made the babies say, *"Shie-shie Da-shu"*—Thank you, Big Uncle. I could not help laughing and started to call her *Da-shu*.

The train smelled like an animal cage. There were hens and ducks in nylon fishnets under the seats by our feet. The locals brushed the leftovers from their bowls onto the floor for the animals. No one bothered to clean up the animal shit. People smoked and chatted loudly. Katherine and I sat facing each other. She was reading *The Three Kingdoms*, a book about the strategies of

Han Dynasty warlords that Mao prized. I was impressed with her endurance.

I turned to watch the landscape out the window. "Great China, my motherland . . ." I thought of the song I used to sing when I grew up. "Beautiful China, pearl of the sea, star of the East." Now the words sounded empty. They bored me. I thought about the way Katherine talked about her country, her ideas about art, men, and life.

To Katherine it was everyday talk. To me it was enlightenment. People in China never talked this way, never spoke about personal feelings. They would talk about the Chen family's son marrying the Li family's daughter, hopefully getting a grandson soon; about what herb soups to drink to make sons; about families who had *dai-jia-nu*—daughters-available-for-marriage-but-need-the-male-to-provide-a-room; about how to get a city residency number through a back-door connection; about how to make deals to get a child out of a labor camp; about useful gifts for government officers—cartons of cigarettes, mai tai wines, foreign-made watches; about how to get out of jail if caught corrupting the Party's workers.

People in China did not talk about dreams or pleasure. Lion Head was an exception, but he only talked about his own interests, the revenge he'd take, the unfairness he'd experienced in his youth, about how much society owed him. Of course, Jasmine too was an exception, talking about her forever unsatisfactory life, her eternal disappointment, her hatred, and her powerful but useless father.

I liked to listen to Katherine's beautiful silly dream talk. She would say, "I would like to learn Chinese painting. I would like to

be a filmmaker. I would like to grow Chinese herbs in my backyard." I tried hard to understand who she wanted to be.

The closer we got to our destination, the poorer people looked.
Children's arms were like bamboo sticks; animals looked like
bones wrapped in skin.

Katherine was composing a letter to the director of the orphanage that stated her intention to adopt a child. When she
finished, she read it to me and asked for comments. I told her that
she would never be allowed to adopt with a letter like that.

She looked confused. She asked me to explain. I said: "You
cannot say you would like to adopt a Chinese girl because female
infants are disfavored in this country. Our government would
never swallow that kind of insult."

"So how should I put it?" Katherine scratched out what she'd
written.

"Say you will learn so much of the great Chinese culture from
this child. The child will help educate you."

"That's ridiculous! I'm going to be educated by . . . we're
talking about a baby!"

"It doesn't matter," I said. "The point is that the authorities
only want to hear things that will soothe their ears."

"But I have to be honest," she said.

"You want the child or not?" I said impatiently.

"Oh, the games we play . . . ," Katherine sighed and began
to rewrite the letter.

At two in the afternoon Katherine and I were having lunch in
one of the carriages. The noodles tasted like rubber bands. Katherine ate one spoonful and pushed her plate aside. I was eating

slowly, sinking in my thoughts. Suddenly a pair of chopsticks came from behind and picked some noodles from my plate. I turned and saw the face of a five-year-old boy, dirty, thin, pitiful. He was with no adult. When I turned back, Katherine's plate was gone. I couldn't eat anymore. I gave the boy my plate. Katherine and I went back to our seats. The conductor announced that we were nearing Ningsia Hui Province. Katherine and I got off at Lucky Village in the early evening.

Katherine had a letter from a Shanghai city official which indicated who she was and what kind of help she sought from the village leaders. The next day we asked around about the location of the orphanage. A boy took us to the orphanage and Katherine gave him a piece of chocolate candy. He was thrilled.

Katherine suddenly asked me if she was doing the "right thing." I couldn't answer her. I was more nervous than she was. I had recently learned from a relative who worked in the medical field that China had over one hundred thousand orphans, sixty percent of whom were handicapped or mentally retarded. I thought about how I poisoned my fetus and became very scared for Katherine.

"What's wrong?" she asked.

"Why? Why do you want to adopt?"

She looked at me and said slowly, "I have a lot to give, and I feel rewarded when I do. I always wanted a child of my own and I've been thinking about adopting a baby for years. I know how it feels to be abandoned, I know how to help . . ."

I took Katherine's hand and at that moment felt that we were connected in a deep, God-made way. I felt that we were adopting the child together.

The headmistress of the orphanage did not speak much. She was an old lady of about sixty. Tired-looking. She carefully read through Katherine's documents and took us inside a courtyard. The place looked like an abandoned temple. We looked around and heard babies crying. The woman seemed used to the cries. She concentrated on reading the letters. After she finished, she waved us to follow her through the yard.

"The girls are at lunch," she said. She took us to the dining room. It was dimly lit. There were stoves with huge bamboo steamers on top. A smoke-darkened chimney on the wall. About thirty children sat around rows of long wooden tables, burying their heads in bowls, eating sweet potatoes and porridge. All girls. According to the headmistress, they were between two and twelve years old. They turned to stare at us, like squirrels, holding their bowls by their mouths. They looked afraid, especially of Katherine. Katherine smiled and waved hello with her hand. No one moved or blinked an eye.

We were led to the orphanage's tiny office. Katherine described the type of girl she would like to adopt. I translated for her. I had advised Katherine not to speak any Chinese in order to avoid any miscommunication. She might mean to say "I respect you," but instead it could come out as "I am scared of you."

The headmistress was taking notes. She flipped through the papers and pointed to a name. "This girl will suit you," she said. "Five years old, healthy, good personality."

Katherine said, "May I please see the girl first?" She forgot that she was not supposed to speak Chinese.

"You can only reject after the viewing," the woman said.

Katherine asked, "What does that mean?"

"It means that you cannot choose from a selection."

"Why not?"

"Because we are not selling the children."

"And I am not buying the children," Katherine said emphatically.

"I did not make this policy. I have to go upstairs, please."

Katherine looked upset and frustrated. I suggested that we take a look at that girl anyway. The headmistress told us we could go to the playroom where the children were, and she would be right down.

When we arrived in the playroom, we saw a fierce fight between a girl about six years old who looked like a bully and a younger, thin girl of about four. The bully's ruthlessness shocked us. She cornered the younger girl and kicked her. The small girl screamed without a voice. I heard Katherine say, "Oh my God." And I kicked her to shut her up.

The bully girl pulled the younger girl's hair. She ordered the other girls in the room to join in. The attack was completely animal-like. The younger girl was struggling, fighting silently as she was thrown over tables and against the wall. The girls were giggling as they took turns kicking her. The bully girl grabbed a broom and began to hit the little girl with it. She wrapped her arms around her head and called for help, but no voice came out. "Oh my God, she's mute," Katherine choked out.

She could not bear the scene; she became breathless. "Someone has to do something," she murmured, and was about to break up the fight. I grabbed her arms and told her that this must happen every day and there was not much she could do about it.

"But they're hurting her, don't you see? She's mute and maybe deaf too. This is crazy. I'm not going to stand here and do nothing."

"Yes you are," I said. "Don't be stupid. This is China."

Suddenly Katherine spoke with such emotion in her voice. "I want her to be my child."

I looked into her eyes and saw a strange bright light.

"That's the one I want to adopt."

"But she's dumb, and who knows what other problems she has."

"Maybe I could care less," said Katherine.

The headmistress reappeared. The girls scattered as if nothing had happened. The bully girl put on a sweet face and greeted the mistress with a humble bow. The younger girl stayed in the corner and quietly wiped her tears. She looked like she was used to this type of beating. The headmistress waved Katherine over and introduced her to the bully girl. "This is Mei-mei, the girl I recommend you take for adoption. Look how cute she is. She's my favorite. I really hate to let her go."

Katherine took a step back and tried to smile. She failed. She took a deep breath. "Sure, of course, I can see that," she said as she pinched my thigh. She wanted my help.

I thanked the headmistress for her wonderful recommendation. "Mei-mei indeed is an excellent choice," I said. "But Katherine has a religious problem."

Both Katherine and the headmistress looked at me puzzled. "What's that?" Katherine asked in English.

In English I responded, "You fool, I'm trying to help you."

In her funny Chinese Katherine said: "That's right. It's a religious problem. I am so sorry that I neglected to bring it up during our meeting."

I began making up stories for Katherine. I was nervous, but I made the director believe that because of Katherine's religious beliefs, it would be better if the girl were mute. I told her that Katherine's mother had been mute, so she was sensitive to the special needs of a child unable to speak. Then I said something about how Katherine believed that it was her religious obligation to be the communicator between God and a child, how she was especially devout. I didn't understand it much myself, I told the headmistress, but Americans believed in such things. I spoke for about fifteen minutes. The headmistress seemed vaguely to understand me. Katherine nodded from time to time. I concluded with Mao's teaching about making friends with proletarians around the world. I said that it would be the Party's wish to help Katherine find a mute for adoption, thus uniting the world's proletarians. It would be the orphanage's contribution to the world's revolution.

The headmistress promised to see what she could do to meet Katherine's religious needs. I said that we didn't have much time. We were hoping for a quick decision. The woman said that in fact she did have a mute in the class. She called for the poor little girl Katherine was trying to protect.

"What's her name?" Katherine asked.

"Xiao-tu," Little Rabbit, the headmistress said.

Katherine took Little Rabbit's hands. The girl didn't move; she let Katherine hold her. She gave the bully girl a sideways glance and let her hands rest in Katherine's. Katherine had tears in her eyes. "You will be my baby," she said in English. "Would you like that?" Little Rabbit nodded as if she understood.

The headmistress said, "Let's start the paperwork." Katherine asked how long it would take. The headmistress said at least six months to get all the stamps needed and to investigate Katherine's records and financial situation. "Just routine procedure, nothing to be worried about." Permission was granted Katherine to spend time with Little Rabbit on holidays.

On our way back to Shanghai, Katherine thanked me for making her a "complete human being." She said that she was all of a sudden starving. I took her to a noodle restaurant next to the bus station. The name of the restaurant was the #1 Taste Under Heaven. We ordered two big bowls and Katherine finished hers quickly. "I never had such great noodle soup in my life," she said, and insisted on going to the kitchen to see how the noodles were made. We went out back and peeked through a fence. Hundreds of flies were parked on the dough, breeding.

Lion Head made me paints with egg yolks. When I went to his place to pick them up, he served me tea. He showed me his recent attempts at a "faceless self-portrait." In the photos Lion Head's face looked like the worn sole of a shoe. I thought they were very good.

He began to talk about how he was able to see through the skin to people's hidden natures, like Katherine's, for example. A phony American who was good with her mouth but came from a culture devoid of history was therefore doomed to be shallow.

"I saw how infatuated you were with her in the beginning. How do you explain that?" I asked. He replied that it was only a way to conquer her, and by conquering her he was conquering imperialism. "It was almost a political action."

I reminded Lion Head that Katherine was my good friend.

"But we are Chinese," he said. "We are the better people. We invented the rockets, not them. We are the ones with genius genes." He waved his arms in the air and spoke in a high-pitched voice.

I looked at his small eyes filled with bitter rage. I said: "It's just because you are not tall enough to pick the grapes that you say they are too sour to eat. Your weakness disappoints me."

"You're not on her side, are you?" His voice turned cold. "You don't want to be her running dog, do you?"

I told Lion Head that I thought his heart was only as big as the eye of a needle. "You once told me that your heart was big enough for a ship to sail through. What's happened to you?"

Lion Head looked at me. "Do you despise me?"

I did not say yes.

"Let me tell you something," said Lion Head. "You have a severe psychiatric problem. Truly, the devil is beginning to eat up your mind. I can see how you will be destroyed."

"Save yourself first," I said, getting up to leave.

I saw gifts on the table. Clothes and toys. I told Katherine that she would spoil things by sending Little Rabbit presents. Equality was what this country was supposed to be about. The Cultural Revolution promoted fairness—kids from poor families were allowed to beat kids from rich families because they felt unequal. I convinced her that the gifts would bring more harm and no peace to Little Rabbit.

Katherine took my advice. She told me that the hospital she was sent to for her checkup for the adoption had asked her to come in for another blood test.

"The government wants to make sure you don't have a sexually transmitted disease," I explained.

"Why? That's practically an insult!" Katherine gestured broadly with her hands. "And even if I did, what business is it of theirs and what does it have to do with the adoption?"

"Well, to China, if you have that kind of disease, you are considered a bad person. You are not a good example for the child."

"All right, all right." Katherine tried to breathe evenly. "What else should I be prepared for?"

"I don't know—they might want you to get a letter from the United States police department to prove that you have no criminal record and that you were never involved in selling children before."

"Are you serious? That's absurd."

"Do you want Little Rabbit or not?"

Katherine blinked her eyes at me.

"So you have to deal with the shit. You better sing our song since you are climbing our mountain."

Lion Head told me he had gone with Jasmine and Mr. Han to visit her grandparents. He was officially a soon-to-be-son-in-law.

Lion Head said he was literally thinking about murdering Mr. Han. He told me that he had become sexually abusive of Jasmine because of his frustration. He made her call herself all kinds of horrible names during the act. But she mistook it for love and asked for more. Now Jasmine had to wear a scarf to cover her bruises.

"What can I say? She's a woman in love. Deep down, though, she knows that I am not with her when we're together," Lion Head sighed. "But she is determined to beat me. She's strong-willed that way. She is Mr. Han's daughter. She will win."

Katherine and I sat on stools in front of the hut at sunset. The adoption was going through slowly. Besides the paperwork I'd guessed the government would want, there was one more request to be dealt with: Katherine had to provide a letter of proof that her family had not committed any crimes for "three (must be biological) generations."

"I don't even know my biological parents, let alone my grandparents and great-grandparents, so how am I supposed to come up with this?" Katherine looked at the paper in disbelief.

"Make it up," I suggested. "No one in this government can check on you in America, so why not say whatever will make you look best?"

"Like what?"

The sky became bloodshot. The wild plants were bouncing their heads, giggling in the wind. Katherine was in her brown sweater. She leaned over to watch me prepare her family tree.

"They must be proletarians, of course. Are there peasants in America?" I had been wondering about this for a while.

"Peasants? Well . . . not really. Can't we just say they were farmers or something?"

"No, no, no. 'Farmers' sounds like they were landlords. Who worked for farmers in your grandfather's time?"

"What, slaves? Is that what you're asking?" Katherine wore a strange expression.

"Good! We'll say they were slaves and . . . beggars! That's good." I wrote it down. "Now, one more. What else? We should make it something brave and productive."

"I know!" Katherine said. "Coal miners!"

"Very good." She watched me write it down and bent over her knees laughing.

After I finished the letter, I went to wash my hands in the pond. When I came back, I found Katherine gazing into the long grass. I went to sit next to her and asked softly what was bothering her. She made no answer. I asked if it was that she missed her homeland. She smiled and said that it wasn't about her homeland. It was something else. I asked what it was. "You're going to think it's silly," she said. "But the games Chinese play, it's like chess, every day, watching my every move. It's draining me."

"I wish I could quit too," I said. "But if I quit, I lose. The reality is that I have too little space, can't work, can't relax, can't be alone. Every inch of space I have to fight for. That's China. That's how we've become inhuman. So many mouths to be fed. One is born to be deprived here unless one is strong enough and can play the games well enough. The irony is that we consider ourselves the most civilized nation. We do everything with elegance, including man-eating."

We sat and chatted the evening away. Katherine cooked two bowls of rice. She used the chopsticks well except she held them too close to the bottom. "Do you think I can pass?" she asked.

"For a Chinese? No," I said. "You are not humble enough."

She laughed and went off to clean the kitchen and outhouse. She used to tell me that, as a typical American, she was obsessed with tidiness. Her bathroom had to be spotless. I told her that would be my ideal. But where I lived ten people shared one bathroom. To keep it spotless was like trying to keep one's fingernail from growing. I wondered if there would ever be a chance in my life that I would have my own bathroom. I would keep it neat the way Katherine did hers.

After we made ourselves comfortable in her living room, chewing sunflower seeds with our legs on the table, Katherine asked if I thought we were best friends. She lit dynamite, I thought.

What did she want? Out of nowhere I could suddenly hear Lion Head's voice. I turned to face Katherine, her auburn hair, lynx eyes, vaselike body, a combination of beauty and cruelty. I thought of Lion Head's Chineseness. I couldn't help but picture the two, Lion Head and Katherine, the locked bodies clinging to ivy. I had been trying to bury that image but it shot straight toward my forehead.

"I am sorry," she said. I was sure she had detected my thoughts. But it was too late for me to hold back.

"Would you like to talk about it?" she asked gently.

"What is there to talk about?"

"I was . . . well, I guess everyone has their weak moments . . ."

I interrupted her. "Tell me that you were never attracted to Lion Head. Tell me that you never wanted to have a Chinese man. Tell me you have sought no pleasure in China at my expense. Tell me nothing ever happened between the two of you that afternoon on the mountain, and now tell me we are best friends."

She was cornered in a most awkward position; her mouth opened and closed. She swallowed her saliva.

I stared into her crystal-clear eyes, the color of the Yellow River in the sun's shadow, inlaid with shining spikes of the sunset.

"Can you handle the truth?" she asked.

"I want nothing but the truth, Katherine," I said firmly.

"Look, my regret is beyond a simple apology. All I can say is . . . it just happened. It was one of those things. At the very least it was unethical. What else can I say? I know I've hurt you . . ."

I took in her words, swallowed them slowly, making sure they did not cut me too hard. And still I felt the edge of an invisible knife. "You foreign bitch. You played with him. You didn't care about anything but your own pleasure. You are a selfish animal."

"Say what you want, but remember," she said, "whatever it was, it was between Lion Head and me. It took place for a reason. I excused myself because I thought you didn't love him, or did you? In any case, it doesn't make me feel less guilty either way."

"But it's not about whether I loved him or not." I gulped the words. "It's about how you teased and betrayed me."

"Well, you don't have to make me feel any more terrible than I already do. The truth is that Lion Head and I were once attracted to each other, just like you and he . . ."

"No!" I yelled. "Lion Head hates you!"

"How do you know that?" asked Katherine, almost smiling.

"He told me so," I said. "He told me so last night. He said you were a phony American."

"Oh, well." Katherine sighed. "I guess actions speak louder than words. Do you want me to prove he's a liar? Lion Head and I have a date tonight. Would you care to come along? Only if you can behave civilly, of course."

I stared at Katherine.

"If you decide not to speak to me again, there is nothing much I can do," she said, folding her hands under her armpits.

"I don't know you, Miss America."

"Cut the shit. Nine-thirty tonight at Red Peony Park, in the abandoned Lord Temple behind the olive tree. You'll see who's your friend."

I had a headache. I wandered the streets after I left Katherine's hut and sank myself in the sea of people. I walked without purpose. What would I see tonight? Was there anything more to shock me? I imagined the two bodies ironing each other. Would Lion Head take her home? How did her skin look in the dim light of his room? How would he feel, touching her breasts again, tracing the curve of her waist, smelling her foreign fragrance, and hearing the way she moaned? I thought about Lion Head's excitement and his betrayal of me. I was jealous.

I got on a suburban bus with about a dozen passengers and dozed off until the conductor woke me up at the end of the line. I got off the bus. The moon was riding the wind, passing black clouds at high speed. Thunder rolled in the distance. The universe felt like an ancient stage.

I was in the open fields of the Cha-hua Gardens, the home of a kind of wild mountain rose. They were vast in numbers. The buds bloomed like fireballs during the day. When the flower withers, it tumbles and turns to ashes almost instantly. Happiness and sadness in the same moment. My spirit was lifted by the beauty of the flowers, but I couldn't avoid seeing the *cha-hua* wither. The beauty jumped on my face, took away my breath, and then beat me up. Petals, scattering like snowflakes, piled up at the flowers' roots. It made one feel honored and deprived at the same time. Katherine. Lion Head. I had no way of knowing myself but through them.

I passed the garden's Foreign Friendship Gift Shop. The lady behind the counter called out, "I'm closing," as I stepped into the shop. A banner hung from the ceiling that read PROLETARIANS UNITE! LONG LIVE THE WORLD'S REVOLUTIONARY FRIENDSHIPS! The shop displayed imitation traditional robes to fool China lovers and Peking opera masks, also for fools. Something glittering under the counter caught my eye. I leaned over the counter and looked at the pairs of earrings, stone-shaped, shell-shaped, diamond-shaped. My ears were not pierced. Modern Chinese women no longer did things like that to enhance physical beauty and please men.

My grandmother's feet were like rice cakes, I remembered. I used to sleep holding them. Her crooked toes gave me nightmares. Grandmother told me that her mother made her do that. She was told that no one would marry her unless she bound her feet. I once asked Grandmother how painful it had been. She said that every day she felt like an animal on a slaughtering block. The sharp pain went on for years, from age three to sixteen. The pain didn't stop until her body stopped growing. There were infections. The feet mildewed. It smelled like spoiled porridge. She had to stay in bed most of the time. Her room was full of wrapping cloth. Then, when she was seventeen, men thought she was beautiful. The way she walked—*ruo-bu-jin-feng*, too weak to withstand the wind—made her a perfect beauty. She was married off that same year. Her parents were very proud.

But the pain in her heart never went away. She showed me her right foot. The toes curled into the ball of the foot. She could not walk far. If she did, her feet would hurt and swell. She still remembered her mother's tears as she bound the little feet every day. I would rub my grandmother's ankles. She tried not to show her pain, but I knew she was suffering.

I looked at the earrings, thinking about Katherine. The woman who had no idea what "lotus feet" meant. I couldn't remember whether Katherine had pierced ears. I didn't care. I wanted to buy her the ocean-green pair. I came to terms with the fact that I hated her and loved her too. I wanted to see her wearing my earrings. I wanted to give them to her tomorrow to let her know that at this moment I missed her. I asked the clerk to put them out on the counter. A pair of tiny, delicate jade boots. I asked the clerk to wrap them up.

I could see Katherine and Lion Head sitting together under the hundred-year-old tree in the moonlight. Other lovers wandered around like ghosts pouring hot words into each other's ears. Arms around shoulders. Head-to-head, as if glued together. The fragrance of flowers danced thick and thin in the air.

Katherine and Lion Head. What are you talking about? I hadn't realized until that moment that they had both been my lovers. Logic disappeared. My senses blurred. I felt instinct calling. God in heaven, embrace me with your black velvet cloak.

Katherine and Lion Head were talking. No hand gestures. I could not hear them. It was better that way. The leaves fluttered above their heads. It started to rain. Typical Shanghai rain. Thin and playful.

I saw them get up and shake hands. Lion Head's hair was flat. He said something, his body leaned against the tree trunk, he spoke loudly, made a big gesture, arm traveling through the air until finally he punched the trunk with his fist, angrily. He stood with his back to Katherine, then suddenly he walked away.

Katherine remained seated. She watched him disappear in the mist. Then she turned around, toward my direction. I couldn't see her eyes. I knew she was looking for me. But I didn't make myself seen. I went home.

In the dark hallway that led to the library, I presented my gift. I tried to make it a casual gesture. I said, "Oh, Katherine, how are you? By the way, here's something for you."

She didn't stop walking. She smiled and said, "Oh thanks. What's in the box?" She shook it and passed me without slowing down.

I had carefully wrapped the box with dry leaves glued on straw paper. I was no longer important to her. I wanted so much to tell her that there was a pair of beautiful earrings in the box; that Chinese women never wore earrings; that I wanted us to be best friends; that they cost me a month's salary but of course I wasn't talking about money, what I was talking about was . . .

As I watched her back, I felt rejected. There was no reason for her to pay attention to me—as my father would say, to a fool whose brain was made of tofu.

I heard the sound of Katherine's heels. I turned and saw her walking toward me. I was about to walk away. I was afraid that she might do something that would embarrass me. Yet I was curious. I slowed down, allowing her to catch up, and felt her hand tap me on the shoulder.

"You didn't have to do this." Her voice was soft.

"I wanted to," I said, feeling a little dizzy, as if walking on a cloud.

"Why?" Her voice was softer still.

My words stuck in my throat. I made an effort, took a deep breath, and pushed the syllables up. Imagining a pair of chopsticks prying open my jaw, I fired out the words. I heard myself say, "Because we are friends."

"That's nice of you, thank you," she said in a pleasant tone.

I shut my eyes.

She walked away, swaying her buttocks.

I never saw her wear that pair of earrings.

My aunts came to visit the family. Aunt Golden Moon and Aunt Silver Moon were talking secretly with my mother, showing her photos. When I came in the room, they looked at me from head to toe, then smiled excitedly at each other. I·tried to ignore them. I knew my mother had been worried about my age and my declining price on the marriage market.

I didn't want to face the fact that my womanhood was depreciating every day. It would have been dishonest to say that I wanted to live by myself till the end. I didn't have much time left to pretend. The truth was going to get me. Once I passed thirty, the neighbors would look at me with pity in their eyes. The matchmakers would keep offering men but they would get older and uglier.

My mother was losing her inner strength. Though she initially refused, she began to look at the photos my aunts presented. She tried to find a son-in-law among them. In the meantime, she watched me nervously.

I felt dutiful toward my family. I was afraid of missing the "only opportunities left," as my aunts cautioned me. "At least make a date with a gentleman—magic might happen," they said.

———

On my way to the date, on a bus, I studied the man's photo in detail. He was in his early thirties. An ordinary face. Round. Seemed nice. He taught mechanics at Shanghai Industrial University. He was from the North and was supposed to be big and tall. My mother must have told my aunts that I couldn't stand to be with a man shorter than I.

I put the photo back in my pocket and forgot the man's face. I took it out again. Studied it. Put it back. I did this several times. I simply couldn't memorize the man's face. I said to myself, Let him do the work. If we both failed to recognize each other, that would be that.

He recognized me, but I couldn't believe my eyes. It was the way he carried himself that shocked me. He moved like a sea lion, as if he had a big heavy tail. He dragged and swayed his bottom half as he walked. He was tall but had short legs. He carried a black plastic document bag on his shoulder which tipped him to the right. "Hello," he said. "Have you eaten?"

I said I hadn't. He said he would take me out to dinner. He took me to the university cafeteria and bought me a box dinner of fried rice with beans. I never liked fried rice with beans. He bought himself a box dinner too. His was rice with chicken. He said no words to me. He just ate and ate like a pig, with a loud shoveling noise. He didn't look at me. After he finished eating, he wiped his greasy mouth on his sleeve. Then he sat and waited for me to finish my food.

I had a hard time eating. I was so disappointed. With a stuffed mouth I stood up and went to empty my box in the leftover vat by the cafeteria door. When I came back to the table, he said, "Would you like to meet again?"

I had my family on the floor with the way I described my date. My brother was greatly amused. My father shook his head and turned to look at my mother. My mother looked sad, but she couldn't help laughing too. Mother asked what exactly was wrong with the man. I said, "Nothing. It's just that I can't help laughing when I think of him."

"But this is a good sign," she said. "You can keep each other amused!"

"Mother," my brother yelled, "don't you see? He's a clown in her eyes!"

A month later I went on another date. He was the son of my aunt's colleague at the hospital. From a good family. The family had grace, my aunt told my mother; they were educated abroad. The son was one year older than me. He was a dubbing actor and had a good voice. He dubbed for movie actors who didn't have a good voice or didn't speak well. He was famous in this circle.

A toothless lady called my name from the phone booth down the lane. Now every neighbor would know that I had gotten a phone call from a young man named Wu. Heads popped out of each window as I walked out in my slippers to make a return call from the booth. I walked lazily, pretending the call was not a big deal. My mother didn't say anything when I paid a three-cent service fee to the toothless lady. Mother watched me with deep seriousness in her eyes. I knew she was praying again.

"Hello?" I heard a voice like a banjo on the other end. He sounded like Mr. Perfect.

"Saturday?" I said. "Sure . . . A walk after dinner? Sure . . . Seven o'clock? Sure."

He showed up at seven o'clock sharp. Neatly dressed. A

square face. Leather jacket and nice pants. He offered to shake hands with me. A comrade handshake. He had skinny, pale white hands. "Let's walk."

The banjo played. For ten blocks. I listened carefully and tried hard to fight my boredom. Although he was an army veteran, his life had been easy. Luck had been with him. So many relatives wanted to fix him up with women. "Too bad that, one way or another, one has to get married," he said.

So he was giving it a try. He was looking for a shoe that fit. He was in no hurry. "Men in their thirties are at their best, which happens not to be the case for women," he said.

"True," I responded, as if aging had nothing to do with me. I wondered whether in America this would be such a devastating problem. I wondered if Katherine ever had to face this in her life.

My feet were begging to take me home. The Wu man offered me a piece of chocolate. It cost him a half day's salary. Now I had to be polite. I dragged myself another two blocks, then I said, "It's getting late, my parents are waiting up."

He said, "Sure, it's been nice. When would you like to meet again?"

I thought for a while and told him that I didn't know.

"How about the day after tomorrow?" he asked.

I said I would be too busy.

"A week from now?" he asked.

"I don't know," I said.

"Two weeks?" he said, his face longer.

"Two months," I said.

He said he understood and we parted at the entrance to the lane. The neighbors turned their heads as I walked by.

I could see my mother leaning out the window, waiting for good news. I felt terrible.

The Party chief, Mr. Han, wanted to have a talk with me, so I hurried to his office. He spit out tea leaves he had been chewing and said: "I am appointing you chairman of the Workers' Union. You have our Party's and the people's trust." A little lost, I asked what the job required of me. He said: "You will assist the Party. Be my extra pair of eyes. Make sure no one disobeys Party rules. You'll submit a twenty-page report to me every Monday."

Party chiefs controlled everyone's life in China and their words were unwritten law. Today one could be named "a hero of the people," and tomorrow, with the chief's mood swing, the hero could be thrown in jail as an "enemy of the people." In order to control the masses, many such "eyes of the Party" jobs were invented. There was a long chain of command—from national political security guards down to the "three-foot detectives," a neighborhood watch retired men and women joined. Since the Communist liberation in 1949, "the network" had become a powerful system of communication and enforcement. Chairman Mao's latest instructions or news of a rally could be made known to every household that same day, spread by a word-of-mouth daisy chain. Also, any counterrevolutionary activity could be reported by one's neighbor and the person who violated the law could be executed just as quickly, thanks to the Party's "eyes" in every family.

The job of chairman of the Workers' Union was one of those invented titles. It was not a promotion nor did it change my duties or my "borrowed worker" status at the electronics factory. It was

Mr. Han's way of controlling me by keeping me busy organizing weekly "thought re-brushing" meetings, writing up reports, collecting membership dues (every worker was automatically a member), and getting workers to subscribe to the Party's *Red Flag* magazine.

I was assigned to the job right after Jasmine's second suicide attempt. Mr. Han had discovered that his daughter was secretly collecting rat-poison pills and writing obsessive love letters to Lion Head. He made sure every possible source of harm was taken away from her.

I had no say over Mr. Han's decision. I knew he didn't count on someone like me to be his eyes. But in taking an interest in me he was implementing a favorite Party boss tactic, *ran-yin-jian-shi*— use both harsh and conciliatory acts to tame the majority. Mr. Han was letting me know that I was under his wing and under his watch at the same time.

Katherine continued her research on Chinese women. I would see her interviewing people on campus and on the street, I'd see her studying in the library, and I'd see her jogging every morning. Her self-discipline was impressive. She would do cartwheels on the lawn. Her youthfulness and energy, at her age, were surprising to the Chinese.

Katherine again asked to interview me. She wanted me to talk about my new position, how it felt to be the chairman of the Workers' Union.

I told her I had nothing to say about it.

"Is that right?" she said. "Aren't you working for your people?"

I said yes and no. I explained that it was basically a harmless position. She asked me to be more specific. I told her it meant that I wasn't hurting anybody. She pressed me again, said she just wanted to understand what I had to do. I said not everything had to be understood. It was important not to understand certain things in China.

"Well," she said, "I'm an American, what do you expect?"

I told her a famous Chinese saying went, *"Da-zhi-ruo-yu,"* meaning "Smart people make themselves look stupid in order to protect themselves." She said she didn't mind looking stupid, she just wanted to be sure she was smart. She said she didn't like to feel confused. I told her another Chinese saying: "The bullet hits the first bird to stick his head out of the nest."

Katherine said that she was starting to see what China was all about. China was a big rusty machine with too many bad screws.

"That's right," I said. "And I am one of those screws."

She thought that wasn't a healthy attitude. "China will be ruined if its people stop caring."

I corrected her. "China is not alive."

She sighed and said, "I hope down deep this is not what you believe."

"You bet I do."

She looked at me and went silent. Finally she said: "Well, one thing's for sure. I don't see China the way you do. I see it as a part of the larger world. We're all here on the same planet, we're all in this together. You, me, everyone."

She was sitting on the front steps of the building. Her head was tilted to the side and she was squinting because the sun was on her. She wore no makeup. Her skin was terribly pale. She looked peaceful. I envied her that look. Some students passed us by. They walked quickly with their heads lowered. They had a bitter appearance, faces made crooked by eternal anxiety. I was sure I looked even worse.

The sky began to turn purple. The clouds were in a fishskin pattern. "Tomorrow is going to be a beautiful day," she said, her voice full of hope.

I looked at Katherine; my mind stopped thinking.

A male student was playing a cassette under a nearby tree. He hummed with the song:

> I am asking the passing cloud,
> Where are you going?
> I'd like to ride the wind, chasing after you,
> Go wherever you are going.

My new boss at the electronics factory handed me a letter to sign. He told me I could either quit school or be put on the factory's "flexible list," meaning I could lose my job at any moment. The factory was in the process of "reorganizing" its workers, to conform to the "one carrot, one slot" effect; no one was permitted to have a do-nothing, Mao-era job anymore.

I signed the letter and put my name on the "flexible list." I saw no other choice. To quit school meant giving up any possibility of change, and giving up Katherine. I had to stay in school. Besides, it didn't make much difference; I was still a "borrowed worker" without a hu-ko in any case.

Lion Head and I no longer slept together but we had become better friends. I was able to accept him for who he was now that he was not my lover, which made things much easier between us. I went on photography trips with him and learned a lot about the camera. His selfishness was inseparable from his intelligence. I spent time with him behind Jasmine's back. He went to Jasmine for sex. "Jasmine has to be mated five times a week," Lion Head told me. He liked talking to me about the way he had sex with Jasmine. I liked listening because he was so incredibly egotistical, conceited, and spoiled. Sometimes I thanked God for getting me out of the affair. He said that Jasmine was a super bed partner and that was all he needed from her. He asked whether I knew of a western magazine called *Playboy*. When I said no, he suggested I ask Katherine about it.

I ran into Jasmine in and out of class. She seemed happy and suspicious at the same time. Her taste in clothes was improving, thanks to Lion Head. She no longer tried to dress like a doll. She wore more sophisticated clothes and tried to match the colors Lion Head wore. Although Lion Head didn't treat her with respect, he no longer pushed her arm away when they walked together. She could hardly believe Lion Head was being faithful and was even more obsessed with him each passing day. She spoke with joy of Lion Head's wild and endless desire.

"He loves to have me beg him to take me," she would tell all her girlfriends. "So I beg him. Then he makes me hit myself with the sole of my shoe . . ."

Lion Head needed Jasmine's body. He didn't want to commit, but he was too selfish to leave. He thought if he left things the way they were maybe at some point in the future he would be able to break away. But Mr. Han was no fool. He wanted to nail him down as a son-in-law or no more free meals for Lion Head. Mr. Han was pressuring Lion Head to make up his mind. Lion Head knew he didn't have much time before he had to sell himself or be slaughtered. He hated Mr. Han for forcing him to be

Jasmine's male concubine, but he could take no revenge. Lion Head was a cockroach on a kitchen counter Mr. Han could crush any time he got too naughty.

Katherine had become even more popular on campus. She had made some good friends among the students and peasants. Her notebook was getting thicker. The school paper praised her as the "best-loved foreign lecturer." I would visit her from time to time, when I got off work or had finished my union chores. I had a hard time getting her to accept my negative views of my people and country. She would wave me away if I asked her not to trust her new "good friends." She thought I was jealous because she wasn't spending enough time with me. I gave up warning her about China. In a way, maybe she was right; what was the point of worrying about whether the sky might or might not fall on her head?

In fact, I was a little jealous of the time she spent with others, like Little Bird. Little Bird was such a plain girl, not interesting at all. But Katherine seemed to like everybody. She only came to me when she had questions about the adoption process. Recently she was asked to provide two recommendation letters from local Chinese. Lion Head and I spent a whole day writing our letters.

One week before July 1, the anniversary of the Party's founding, the school authorities began to plan a celebration rally. Lion Head talked to me about how to make the rally our party instead of Mr. Han's. I told him that the Workers' Union, the Student Union, and the school paper had been gathering suggestions from the masses on how best to celebrate the day. Many suggested that Katherine be involved. Without even asking her, the student leaders sent a proposal to Mr. Han and the Party committee suggesting Katherine be included in the program to introduce us to American music. Including Katherine would be our direct response to the Central Bureau's call to enhance communication between East and West. We would get to know America in order to exceed America. Lion Head and I collected newspaper clips on the new "open-door policy" and sent them to Mr. Han's office to show that having Katherine participate would be politically meaningful.

After a couple of days Mr. Han was finally convinced and agreed to the idea.

The student leaders came up to Katherine after class. We asked her to prepare a musical performance. Katherine said she couldn't, she would be too nervous. We begged her. We said we loved the way she danced and we would like to learn more. She would enlighten and educate us through music. She blushed. We pleaded with her until she said, "Maybe."

Katherine asked us to let her think it over for a few minutes. She shut herself in the classroom and paced the floor. When she came out, she asked if we thought the rally was going to be any fun. We screamed, "Yes!" and she said, "Okay."

"I need you." Katherine pointed at me as my classmates were leaving. "On the day of the rally, come to my hut three hours before it begins, okay?"

I nodded and asked, "What do you want me to do?"

"Paint me."

"I have good paints," said Lion Head.

"We don't need him, do we?" Katherine said, half-smiling.

"As you please." Lion Head looked like a wounded animal. He walked away without another word.

"He loves you," I told her.

Katherine put her hands up to her cheeks and opened her eyes wide. "How nice!" she said. "Eating from a bowl and looking at a wok. Actually I don't wish him any harm."

"By the way, what is the magazine called *Playboy*?" I asked.

"Why do you ask?" Katherine said cautiously.

"Lion Head told me to ask you about it. I'm just curious."

"I can get you one from the western community, if you want."

"Never mind," I said.

"Arrrgh!" Katherine made an animal sound and shook her head.

"What?" I looked at her.

"You guys are weird."

"I don't need you to tell me that," I said.

July 1 was a golden day. The flowers of the *fu-yong* trees wagged in the wind like pink tongues. I arrived at Katherine's hut three hours before the event began. She was waiting for me.

I was mute with happiness. She took me to her bedroom. I opened my bag and spread the paints and brushes on her dressing table. She said she was going to wear a black lace bra, and wanted a white peony painted on the front of her chest and a big red peony on her back, and leaves and daisies painted across her shoulders and arms. She would wear a sheer Chinese dress over it all, but the shape of her body and the paint would show through.

She said she was going to "dress to kill."

She lay on her stomach on a bamboo mat quietly. There was magic in my pen. I could see the peony taking shape on her body. I traced its shape. One petal, two petals, the stem, the heart. I felt like a bee sucking a flower. I made little strokes, little strokes, patiently. I touched my brushes to her ivory skin. One hour passed, two hours, the room felt outside of time. I could hear nothing but her heartbeat.

The sun was high, the curtains drawn. I got up to open them to let the light shine on her naked body. She didn't move. Her eyes were closed as if she were sound asleep. I powdered her back to make sure the paint stayed on the skin. I turned her over onto her back. I moved her hips toward me and rearranged her arms. She let me be in charge of her body.

I poured myself chrysanthemum tea and began to draw again. My body was floating. I kept shading the peony petals. My brush moved faster, my hands were sweating, my body tense. Her lips became rosier. I had to touch her. My painting became wild. The blooming peonies were lavish and ripe.

Katherine walked to the mirror with her eyes still on me.

"Tell me I don't look stupid," she said. She looked in the mirror and drew in her breath. "Well, well, well."

As I began to clean up, she came over to me, her arms outstretched. She pulled me close, ironed me with her body, then pressed her lips on my cheek. "I love it," she whispered. "Thank you."

Lion Head came through the door, camera in hand. Katherine looked first at him, then at me, as if to say, Who invited him?

"I did," I said. "Please forgive me. I asked him to record this for me."

"Why?" Katherine went to put on a robe.

I hesitated for a moment, then confessed, "One more day

with you means I have one less day with you. I know it sounds silly, but the photos will be a souvenir after you've gone back to America. When I think of you, I can . . ."

"Jesus Christ, you Chinese really plan death ahead of time, don't you?" she said. "Come on. Let's get it over with."

The sun shone through the leaves into the room. Lion Head moved around looking for the perfect light and angle. Katherine took off her robe and lay down naked on the bamboo mat as I began to paint again. My thoughts were busy. I knew Katherine could care less about Lion Head being there, but I cared. I invited him over because I knew he wanted to be here. I knew he was obsessed with this foreign body. I encouraged him because I wanted him to have as many memories of her as I did, so I would have someone to talk to when I missed her. In this way Lion Head and I had a true marriage, one which Katherine would never understand. I was no less selfish than he; we used each other, helping one another preserve these moments in our incomprehensible lives.

She lay there like a statue. The shape of her body, the flowers on her skin, the beauty of Katherine stunned me. Lion Head looked composed but he was breathing heavily. We didn't say anything. We couldn't. We moved slowly and quietly, like ghosts. Each second carved a deep stroke on the tablet of our memory. We were silent, because we were reading God's poetry with our hearts.

Lion Head motioned to me to cover Katherine with the lace curtains. He wanted me to expose her breasts but cover the nipples. I went to work decorating Katherine. I tried to wrap the curtain around her, but her nipples kept popping out.

"Use tape," Lion Head suggested.

I tried to tape the curtains over her nipples but after a few seconds they would pop out again. Katherine began to giggle. My fingers were busy trying to tame the nipples with tape. Katherine laughed harder. I told Lion Head that the nipples would stay put for about three seconds. The best way to do this was to have me hold the curtains against her nipples while he focused the camera, then I would let go right before he took the picture.

We were late. The rally had already begun. The Party chief was delivering his monumental speech. A crowd of two thousand—students, faculty, and relatives—gathered in the hall, dressed mostly in gray and blue Mao suits. They stood listening to Mr. Han over the loudspeakers. His speech was made up of quotations from the Party's newspapers and magazines. Never in his life had he spoken in public without using quotations. His mind was so filled with quotations, there was no room for his own thoughts. He didn't believe in thoughts anyway because they were dangerous. In China there was only one way to think. Mr. Han once referred to himself as the "red tongue of the Party's propaganda machine."

Foamy saliva formed in the corners of his mouth as he spoke loudly into the microphone. The audience put up with him because they were waiting for Katherine. But they were growing impatient. It was getting noisy. Mr. Han turned up the volume of his microphone. People were paying no attention to him. Suddenly the hall went quiet. Katherine appeared at the entrance to the hall escorted by Lion Head and me. The chief lost his crowd completely.

Katherine covered her painted body with a black coat; still a part of the painting showed through her collar. She wore her hair short and curly. Her makeup defined her sculptural features. She was in high-heeled black suede boots that made her look taller and thinner than usual. She walked in with her head lowered, trying not to distract the crowd from the chief's speech, but no one could take their eyes off her. Lion Head and I pushed the crowd away, but they swarmed in like bees.

Mr. Han continued his speech. "Our advance is firm and our achievements remarkable. We are in control of our society's super-structure and ideology. Our people are determined to devote themselves to the great Communist future. We are opening our-selves to the world and welcoming all positive energy to join us . . ."

Katherine slid into a seat in the section for the foreign lectur-ers to the right of the stage. Lion Head and I went to sit with our class to the left. Jasmine came to take off Lion Head's jacket.

Mr. Han paused at the end of his speech. He was waiting for the crowd to clap their hands. But there was no reaction. He had been totally forgotten. The color of his face changed from red to blue. Lion Head noticed and immediately began to clap. The crowd followed, but all eyes were still on Katherine. The clapping grew louder and louder. Mr. Han's face became a balloon. He was confused. His secretary, a rat-faced man, came and poured him a cup of water as he whispered to the chief.

The men looked at Katherine with animal delight. Jasmine stood next to Lion Head. She watched the way Lion Head looked at Katherine. She bit her lips. She pretended Katherine did not exist. She was on the verge of tears.

"My speech is concluded," Mr. Han said, and the crowd cheered. The rat-faced secretary came up to the microphone and

announced that the entertainment was about to begin but there
was a small change in the program. There was not enough time
for the American portion.

At first the crowd was stunned, then they screamed. The noise
was so loud it seemed like it would break through the ceiling. The
crowd demanded the traditional lion dance be cut. The secretary
on stage became mute. He went to the back of the stage, con-
ferred with Mr. Han, and returned to the microphone. He lifted
his hands above his head in a pose of surrender and said, "All
right, the people's voices have been heard. The American portion
will stay on the program."

The sound of hands clapping and feet stomping was like a
summer rainstorm.

Jasmine's face twisted into a knot.

It was the strongest beat we had ever heard in our lives. The
rhythm woke up our long-sleeping nerves. Our bodies took off.

Katherine came onstage and gave us an introduction to popular music. Rock and roll, rhythm and blues, Motown, funk, and
soul.

At first we listened quietly—it was too overwhelming for us
even to react. Katherine played the music and translated the lyrics
for those who couldn't understand. With the words and music in
sync, we were carried away. The music slowed and a rich voice
wailed. Speaking the phrases soulfully in Chinese, Katherine told
of a "natural woman" whose life was redeemed by another.

I let my tears run freely, let the song soothe my wounded
soul. Many in the crowd stretched their arms out to Katherine.
She smiled. She came offstage to join us on the floor. Lion Head
took her arm and pulled off her jacket. Her painted body showed

through the sheer top. The crowd formed a circle around Katherine and she began to dance to a song with a faster beat. The woman's singing made us want to scream.

I sang along loudly. I couldn't follow the words but I didn't care. The crowd was chanting in ecstasy, even Jasmine. The woman's voice, Katherine's electrifying movements—these sounds and images entered the rusty ancient Chinese minds and gave birth to new brain cells.

Katherine switched tapes and called out, "Listen! This is Mick Jagger and the Rolling Stones." The peony body moved in a slow motion. My eyes burned with what I saw. I felt my heart sweat and let the rhythm carry me. Others around me began to do the same, letting their bodies go, nervously, yet with delight.

Lion Head had his eyes on the foreign body like flies on a butcher's flypaper. He began to scream. Jasmine elbowed him, trying to get him to look away, but his brain was gone. His eyes were half-closed, as if deeply drugged. Jasmine pulled at his sleeve.

Big Lee, Little Lee, and Little Bird were clapping their hands and slapping their thighs. They tried to imitate Katherine, but danced like stiff puppets.

Jim was out of his mind. He threw himself down on the floor, flailing his limbs. He was gone. His newlywed wife, a heavy woman, was embarrassed and came to pick him up, but was dragged down by him. Jim rolled on top of her as they wrestled on the floor.

The crowd was vibrating. Up and down, our minds jumped along with our bodies. Inside of me a fever rose. I felt like I was being thrown around on a ship. The tide was coming in, the water was rising higher and higher, anxious to tear me from my native land. The sails were raised. Katherine, your storming spirit has awakened me. You caressed me with your auburn hair and lost me in your endless flow of night and day. I am breaking away!

We were being transformed, moment by moment. Our hopes were vertical. Our future lay coiled in hearts that were climbing toward the sky. To the past we raised our arms in farewell. A new era was beginning to dawn with a horse-shaped cloud under its feet.

Outside the hall the rhythmic beating of *tong-gu*, the giant Chinese drums, had begun. We surged through the doors. A string of flowers opened in the purple velvet sky. In joy our hearts shouted: Offer me more fire to drink, burn me to ashes, and hear my everlasting cry: Love and freedom!

Surprisingly Mr. Han had no official reaction to the fever aroused at the celebration rally. Maybe it was because Jasmine was there too, or maybe he didn't realize the extent of what Katherine's performance had done to our minds. But perhaps he was thinking of the old saying, *Yu-qing-gu-zong*—In order to tighten the leash, the hunter first lets it loose.

The days brought us closer to graduation. Everyone's future was at the mercy of the Party committee. The first choice was to be assigned to work in Shanghai, anywhere in Shanghai, to become a permanent resident. The worst possibility would be for a "borrowed worker" simply to be returned.

I didn't know what to do. The electronics factory had phased me out after I had signed the paper that put me on the "flexible list" because I wanted to continue my schooling. I was living off my last savings. My parents did not hold powerful city positions and could bring no benefit to the chief or his family in exchange for a favor. I didn't have enough money to buy him gifts like ginseng, wine, or pearl powders. It felt as if someone had taken away the floor and I was falling, waiting to hit bottom.

Like most of the graduates, I moved into the school dormitory. It was a treat for graduating students. It enabled them to study long hours in the library for final exams. Katherine also moved in to help the students with their nightly studies. The dormitory was built like a military barracks, with security guards on duty. The rooftop was my favorite spot. Our school was located on the edge of the city, in a very primeval-looking landscape surrounded by bushes and rice paddies. I often came up to the roof just to think.

Katherine once said to me, "Every time I want to just drop out of life, I do this . . ." She was standing in front of a brick wall covered with ivy. She was in a grass-colored sweater. Holding her right hand to her chest, her eyes shut tightly, she said, "Please, please let it go." She opened her eyes, turned toward the open field, took a deep breath, and wailed wildly.

The sound was terrifying. It pierced my ears. I could see white beams shooting out in front of me. I had never heard such a sound in my life, like a wolf howling at the moon. It brought to mind prehistoric times, primitive animals, a thunderclap.

Katherine said in America some people used this method to release anxiety. She asked me to try it. I felt too funny to do it. I could not bring myself to wail. I could not picture myself acting like an animal.

I told Katherine that I didn't need it. "Chinese are good at handling their emotions," I said.

She did not insist. She smiled and said, "As long as you're in control, you are your own master."

I thought of the songs we sang at the rally. My growing sensitivity softened my character as it weakened my will. I felt like a burned-out candle with wax tears coating my heart's altar.

We were a few weeks away from graduation. I had gone to check at the electronics factory to see if there was any chance of being reinstated, but I found that my name had already been terminated. I was a lamb under a butcher's knife. At night I dreamt of Mr. Han's hideous eyes and his mouth pronouncing my name and woke up in a cold sweat.

The villagers had begun drying their goods, shipping them to food markets in exchange for city products such as plastic containers, fabric, and cheap watches. From the roof I could see the narrow muddy path toward the city jammed with humans, donkeys, and cows.

I sat by myself. The sun was swimming in and out of a sea of clouds. I was imagining my next life, thinking how much I would like to come back as someone like Katherine.

Was Katherine's life any easier? She used to say that all her life she had fought for what she wanted. She called herself a pathological optimist. It had been her dream to come to China to do the book. It was her love of Chinese culture and the people that made her stay. She didn't see that Mr. Han was growing more and more irritated by her behavior. Besides the bold interviews she conducted on campus, her suggestion to change the textbook, of which Mr. Han was the creator, annoyed him. I told Katherine that if she were a Chinese her life would have been finished long ago. She laughed me off and said that I was overreacting.

I stopped trying to make Katherine see people my way, because I didn't like to hear her say that my distrust was destructive. I grew up reading Party bosses' faces; I knew what they were capable of. My father's life was proof that to trust a Party boss was to dig one's own grave. Yet Chinese life was filled with Party bosses. I only wish I knew how to make the sun shine on my head, like Lion Head. He flattered Mr. Han shamelessly. If Mr. Han asked him to lick his spit, he would.

But I didn't want to be Lion Head. I wanted to be Katherine. "In the garden of our great socialist country, flowers like Katherine only exist as decoration, for propaganda pictures, not for changing people's minds," Lion Head said to me after the rally. Of course Katherine had gone beyond the Party's line. She had changed us. I saw heroism in Katherine. I worshiped her. I was sure that most of my classmates felt the same, but it didn't mean much, because we had too much fear, and fear made us impotent.

Jasmine had had a big fight with Lion Head after the rally. She drank down *dee-dee-wei*—rat poison—and was rushed to the hospital emergency room. Mr. Han hurried to his daughter's bedside. He watched the doctors pump her stomach and watched her vomit blue liquid. The Party boss broke down. He threw away his official posture and sat outside the emergency room crying loudly. He said that life had treated him unfairly. He had lost his first wife during the war, his second wife during the Cultural Revolution, and now his daughter was trying to kill herself. He was determined to save her, because she was his one and only seed.

When Jasmine was sent to the recovery room, Mr. Han shut everyone else out. He watched over her day and night. Like a witch casting a spell, he got on his knees and poured words into her ears. He didn't stop for meals or sleep. A nurse turned away people who came to visit Jasmine and told them that the father and daughter had a spiritual bond.

It was in the hospital, in pain, through her father's whispers, that Jasmine completed her transformation from worm to moth, from weeper to warrior.

I visited Lion Head and asked what happened between him and Jasmine. He admitted that he had been having trouble "bedding" Jasmine. "The sight of her body turns me off," he said. "It's not me, it's just my body that shut down on her."

"She must have assumed you were having affairs," I said.

"She's mad. She hates everything. She could eat you and Katherine alive. You think I can stop her? I can't. Go and take a look at how her claws scratch the air."

The thought of Jasmine vomiting blue rat poison made me laugh with guilt. But I knew she would make sure someone paid for her suffering.

Katherine refused to hear me talk about Jasmine's battle drums. She said she was sympathetic to Jasmine's lovesickness. When Jasmine got out of the hospital, Katherine bought a pot of red bamboo from a peasant and sent it to Jasmine's sickbed. She told me both father and daughter had been quite appreciative of her gift. I said to Katherine that it was just a show.

"Oh, come on." Katherine raised her hand in the air, making a stop sign. "You've got to give people a chance. I'm not a child. Let me use my own judgment and common sense."

The Moon Festival came. There were cake-making celebrations in the surrounding villages. Ever since the Liberation, no Chinese treated such days with importance, because they were considered the dregs of feudalism. I didn't bother to go home to eat my mother's moon cakes. I wasn't in the mood. The full moon was supposed to be a symbol of completeness, harmony, and happiness, but I looked at my life and found nothing to celebrate.

People walked home carrying bottles of wine and beer. I didn't drink much but tonight I decided to drink to forget my misery. I got myself a small bottle of Green Bamboo wine and went to sit on the roof with the moon. After a while I began to feel light-headed as I stared at the bright moon.

As the night deepened, I felt every one of my cells begging to cry. I was trying to fight off an acute depression. I noticed a figure moving toward me hurriedly from the other end of the roof. It was my roommate Little Bird.

Little Bird threw herself at me and said loudly, "The *yang-ren* is drunk! Go and take a look! It's quite a monkey show! They are pouring wine into her!"

I snapped out of my mood, got up, and followed Little Bird off the roof.

Big Lee and Little Lee's room on the second floor was filled with people. Everyone was laughing and smoking, standing around a table covered with beer and liquor bottles. The show was on. The leading players were Jasmine and Katherine. Jasmine was holding Katherine's jaw with one hand and pouring liquor into her throat with the other. Smiling, she said in Chinese, "Peony K, you have been such a good teacher, you must accept our warmest regards. That toast was from Big Lee. And now, Little Lee wants you to accept his toast. You can't turn him down, or he will lose face."

Katherine waved away the drink with her hand.

"You must honor Little Lee. It is unfair for you as their teacher to refuse."

"Toast! Toast!" Everybody cheered.

Katherine smiled drunkenly. She was in a black dress that left her shoulders bare. Her hair was messy. She looked beautiful, but she was not herself. Red-cheeked, she was half-lying on Jim's thigh, like a fat snake.

Jim was enjoying himself. He laughed with the crowd, but

made sure his arms accidentally touched Katherine's breasts. He let Katherine's bare arms hang around his shoulders. He was her pillow. He allowed her shaking hand to spill wine on her dress so her nipples showed through. The men's eyes were shining.

"Now tell us, what do you think of the chief?" said Jasmine.

Katherine made an effort to sit up. "Would you all stop pouring me liquor after I answer this question?"

"Sure," everyone said.

"All right," said Katherine. "To tell you the truth, I don't have much respect for Mr. Han. He's not an honest man. He's superficial—extremely and disgustingly so. Basically, I think he's a jerk." She laughed and dropped her glass.

The crowd cheered her on.

Jim tapped Katherine on the shoulder. "A true Communist like Mr. Han fears nothing. Go on, Katherine."

Jasmine smiled. Pointing at Katherine, she said quickly in Chinese, "She is an anti-Communist to the core."

Lion Head came through the room. "Hey, enough is enough," he said. "You know your father would be upset by this. Now stop it."

"What's the matter with you?" Jasmine yelled at Lion Head.

"Look, the foreign devil is drunk," Lion Head replied.

"We should be glad the devil is spitting out the hidden truth."

"But it's unethical to trap a person when she is not quite herself."

"Trap? Who is trapping whom? What do you mean by 'trap'? Why are you so concerned? Huh?" Jasmine looked at Lion Head angrily.

"Truly, I am not that drunk," said Katherine. "And by the

way, I am nobody's devil. I don't care whose father Mr. Han is. I don't like him because he is a number-one hypocrite. I'm glad I'm an American, so I don't have to lie like the rest of you. I've been here too long. I need to get out of my shell, to stretch, to breathe, to have fun, simple fun . . ." She reached her hands over her head, stretching her torso from side to side. "You know, to do something like . . ." She turned around and kissed Jim on the lips. "Out of your shell now! You, you, you!" She pointed her fingers at us and laughed.

"What about Lion Head?" Jasmine asked Katherine suddenly. "What do you think of him?"

"As a man, or as a friend, or as a you-know-what? You have to be specific so I can give you the correct answer."

"As a you-know-what," said Jasmine.

"Put on some music, will you?" ordered Katherine. She got up and someone stuffed a tape in a tape player. "May I?" Katherine wrapped her pale white arms around Lion Head's neck, curled herself around him and started to move to the rhythm.

"Do you want me to tell Jasmine what I think of you? Should I be honest? I've had too much wine. My tongue is slippery. The guard has gone off duty. What should I do? Help me, Lion Head, sweetheart . . ."

Lion Head pulled himself away. He walked toward the door, but the crowd would not let him go.

"Don't spoil our fun!" they shouted. Lion Head pushed his way through but was grabbed by Jasmine.

Suddenly Katherine fell to her knees and began to vomit. Jim got down to wipe up the mess. Katherine laughed and said, "I told you it was too much wine. I am so sorry to make you do this.

But you had your fun warming my body, didn't you? Woo, I think the Moon Festival sucks!"

Jasmine would not leave Lion Head alone. She said, "Lion Head, watch the *yang-ren* vomit, watch the foreigner, look how attractive she is!" She began to laugh hysterically.

Katherine lay down on the bed and wiped her mouth with a wet cloth. "Jesus Christ! You know you're welcome to ask more questions. What the hell, it's a special occasion, right?" She reached out for the bottle Big Lee was passing her.

I stood near the door, feeling like I was waking from a dream. I was hoping Katherine would stop, but it looked like she was going to make things messier. She would drink more and criticize the Party and walk straight into Jasmine's trap.

I went up to Katherine, took the bottle away, and said, "Come on, let's say good night to everyone. Let's go back to your room."

The crowd harassed me and pushed me around. "Hey, Zebra, you're not on duty. Get out of here!"

Someone poured beer over me. The crowd laughed loudly. I pulled the tablecloth off the table angrily.

"Look who's here, Katherine!" Jasmine squealed, pointing at me. "Is she your bodyguard, your personal maid, or your concubine?"

Katherine began to smile mysteriously. I was nervous. I didn't know what she would say. I felt unsafe.

"She's everything you can possibly imagine to me," Katherine said.

I turned to her and shouted, "Please shut up!"

"What's wrong with you, honorable chairman of the Workers' Union? Is there a secret we should know? Why are you so panicky?" Jasmine asked. She didn't look like someone who'd been in the emergency room just two weeks ago. She looked like a snake spitting venom.

"Don't be afraid of her. So what if she has a powerful father, that doesn't mean she's better than you." Katherine reached out for me. "Come here, let me tell you how much I adore you and your black marble eyes . . ."

I raised my hand in the air, shut my eyes, and slapped Katherine's face. Left cheek and right cheek. My palm hurt.

The crowd was shocked.

"We are not in a zoo," I said viciously. "And she is no monkey!" I turned to Katherine and said, "Go back to your room."

Jasmine approached with a glass of mai tai. Pushing me away, she said, "If you don't like this, why don't you just leave? Don't be the tiny piece of mouse shit that ruins the whole pot of porridge."

I went to grab Katherine, but she kept saying that it was fine, she didn't want to leave. She said she was having fun. Jasmine made another toast and Katherine fell dead on Jim.

Jim began to rub Katherine from head to toe. He said he had studied Chinese medical massage, he knew which needle points to pinch. He was half-drunk, and this was not a medical massage. He had Katherine's head between his legs.

I saw a shadow appear behind the crowd. My senses told me to act fast. I pulled Katherine by the arm. Lion Head was watching me from the back of the room, standing still. Jasmine held onto Katherine.

Mr. Han's rat-faced secretary came into the room, and

switched the lights off and on to quiet everyone down. He walked through the crowd and ordered everyone to leave.

The night was unusually quiet. After I sent Katherine to bed, I came back to my room. Little Bird was already sleeping soundly. I decided to work on my final paper. I smelled like liquor. I had helped Katherine take off her liquor-soaked clothes and shoes. Jasmine had been at her best tonight. She took advantage of Katherine's kindness and invited her "to drink to the Moon Festival," then had everyone witness Katherine bad-mouth Mr. Han, so there would be enough "criminal evidence" to get rid of her forever.

My mind felt rusty. And my paper was far from finished. In order to show our "great progress," Mr. Han had assigned difficult topics for our final papers. How was I to criticize Friedrich Nietzsche with my year-old English? Exaggerating victories had been part of the Communist tradition ever since the "Great Leap Forward" in 1957. Millions of peasants were dying of starvation as the Party newspaper reported a harvest of "a thousand-pounds-per-acre yield."

Katherine thought Mr. Han's order was ridiculous, but she gave in because to her it was not a matter of principle. "Mr. Han's behavior just shows a lack of experience with how a foreign language should be taught," she said. "He will find out soon enough and hopefully correct himself." In the meantime Katherine would see how far we could stretch. She said she didn't expect our papers to make sense.

My eyes crawled like snails over the text, but I pushed on, checking with the English-Chinese dictionary every five words.

"Now no comfort avails any more; longing transcends a world after death, even with gods; existence is negated along with its glittering reflection in the gods or in an immortal beyond. Conscious of the truth he had once seen, man now sees everywhere only the horror or absurdity of existence; now he understands what is symbolic in Ophelia's fate; now he understands the wisdom of the sylvan god, Silenu: he is nauseated . . ." I checked the dictionary. I was nauseating for sleep. Before I could write down the translation, the pen dropped from my hand, and down my head fell.

I was in a deep sleep when Little Bird woke me. She spoke in a frightened voice. Shaking my bed, she said, "The couple has been caught! Their reputation is ruined!"

"What? What is it?" I opened my eyes in the dark.

"They are locked in her room together, no way out. Jasmine is getting the guards to make an on-the-spot arrest."

"What? What couple?" I saw dawn just beginning to break. I wondered whether Little Bird was having a nightmare.

"Katherine and Jim—they were caught in bed." Little Bird was breathing hard.

"How do you know about this?"

"I got up to pee and heard a noise. I saw Jasmine instructing the guards to block the door."

I snapped out of sleep. I said to Little Bird, "Turn on the light."

"No!" Little Bird went to cover the light switch. "I am scared." Her voice was trembling. "I don't want to get involved."

"All right," I said. "I'm going to check things out for myself."

"If you go, please don't let anyone know that I told you."

I promised her.

Little Bird warned me not to get involved. I told her that it was too late for me not to get involved. I saw the conspiracy; the Party wanted to get Katherine.

"I cannot hear you." Little Bird covered her ears with her hands.

My footsteps on the staircase. There was no light in the hallway. I stumbled toward Katherine's room.

I heard whispers behind every door I passed. Flashlights were switched on. When I reached Katherine's room at the end of the hall, I saw all the lights focused on the doorknob.

Jasmine grasped the doorknob. There were two big security guards behind her with nightsticks in their hands.

Jim's wife, the short, heavy woman, was standing next to Jasmine, sobbing. She had just arrived. She was wearing a jacket buttoned in all the wrong places.

People began to gather in front of the door. They watched silently. With her hand on the knob, Jasmine began to yell: "You evil couple! You are dreaming if you think you can get away from the people's trial! All ways out are blocked. Raise your hands and surrender!"

There was a cry from the room.

Jasmine directed the security guards to get ready, and with a single force, they pushed the door open.

I jumped up behind the crowd to see.

The room seemed dead in the light of dawn. There was a figure lying on the bed to the left. It was Katherine. She seemed to be still asleep. With all the flashlights shining on her face, she tried to open her eyes. She tried to make her body cooperate with her will. Finally she made herself sit up. "What's going on?" she murmured.

"Good performance," said Jasmine.

"What . . . what are you talking about?" asked Katherine.

"Where is the adulterer?" Jasmine shouted.

"What adulterer? What is this?" Katherine rubbed her eyes.

"Get him!" Jasmine ordered two security guards to search the room. They went out to the balcony. There was the sound of wrestling, struggling, a slipper flew out. A few seconds later Jim was tied with ropes and dragged out. He looked like a drawn dog. He was in blue-striped pajamas and wore one slipper. The other slipper was in Jasmine's hand. When Jim saw his wife, he fell to his knees.

"Secure the evidence," Jasmine ordered.

The hallway was filled with people.

Katherine fell back against her pillow and turned over to sleep as if what was going on had nothing to do with her.

Jasmine instructed the security guards to get Katherine up.

Katherine said she had an intense headache and refused to leave her bed.

Jim's wife began to wail loudly.

The crowd was gossiping about what the *yang-ren* must have done to get Jim in bed with her.

Jasmine walked over to Lion Head, whose face was expressionless.

"What happened?" someone called out.

Jasmine began her report. "I saw a shadow duck into Katherine's room when I got up to use the restroom. It was about five o'clock in the morning. I immediately thought, Could someone be trying to rape Katherine? I must do something to stop it. I followed the shadowy figure. When he stopped at Katherine's door, I recognized that it was Jim. What was he doing here? At first I thought he might have come to give Katherine some aspirin to wake her from the alcohol. But I was shocked when I saw that he didn't switch on the light after he was in the room. Comrades, Jim did not switch on the light. What was he doing in the dark? What could he be doing? Or should I say, what could *they* be doing? I realized at that moment that a crime was being committed. Jim has betrayed his wife and our Chinese morality."

The crowd listened in concentration. Jasmine continued: "Jim has been a good comrade all his life until now. Never once had he cheated on his wife. But Katherine, a corrupt character, seduced him, lured him, and turned a good Chinese man into an adulterer. For this I felt deeply sorry for Jim. I felt an obligation to save our comrade from sliding too far. I decided to call the security guards and catch them in the act. It cannot be more obvious that Jim was used."

The crowd buzzed. They began to talk about how selfish Katherine was. Jasmine looked excited. The public focus was where she wanted it. Lion Head walked away in silence. Jasmine waited for the crowd to heat up.

Her eyes searched the crowd. When finally they landed on me, she smiled. Such a vicious smile. I thought I would shoot her if I had a gun. But I tried not to show my disgust. I realized that punishing Katherine was her way of killing a hen to shock the monkeys. She was warning the rest of us not to step on her toes. Her misery allowed no happiness.

In this country, accusing someone of a "private life corruption" was the most effective way to denounce an enemy. "Private life" was a gray area—no facts need be stated. Many such arrests, punishments, and deaths took place during the Cultural Revolution, and even after Mao died, still it was the same. People hadn't changed—would they ever?

I was too selfish to let Katherine be destroyed. Katherine was no longer living her own life. She was living mine too.

My feet were about to step forward. Little Bird's voice was shouting in the back of my head, "Don't get involved!" But I was beyond self-control. I stepped out of the crowd, climbed to the top of the stairs. Raising my voice, I said, "Jasmine, how do you know it was Katherine who seduced Jim? Why not the other way around? How can you even prove that they had physical contact? How do you know it was not just your imagination?"

Jim was in shock. I looked at him and said, "Jim, you can tell us what happened, can't you?"

"But how can I make the Party believe me? Nobody will, nobody . . ." He shook his head and began sobbing. "How can I explain myself?"

"Give us the chance to believe you," I said.

"Who are you to speak like this?" Jasmine yelled at me.

"In the name of the Workers' Union, I ask that we let Jim speak," I replied calmly.

Jim sobbed like a woman. "I didn't do anything with the foreign devil," he said.

The crowd whistled in disbelief. Jasmine jumped on him. "Then explain—why did you go to Katherine's room? Furthermore, why did you not turn on the light? Why? Confess!" She was looking at me as she spoke.

Jim turned to me as if asking whether he should go on.

I nodded at him in encouragement.

Jim said in a small voice: "She . . . she was so drunk at the party last night, I wanted to bring her some medicine to keep her from vomiting. I got some pills from Jasmine and I told her that I was going to take some and give the rest to Katherine. I didn't go last night because I was drunk myself until I woke up this morning. I went to her room to give . . . to give the medicine. I can't explain why . . . I did not turn on the light. I don't know . . . it felt good being in the dark and . . . and . . ."

"And what?!" shouted Jasmine.

Jim choked. His shame was dreadful.

I said, "We are human. Anybody can have a weak moment."

Jasmine gave me a make-your-dog-stop-farting look.

She had no effect on me. I said to Jim, "Go on please. We should not be ashamed of the truth."

"And . . . and . . . to be near her . . . just near her." Jim spit out the words in exhaustion.

"Be near who?" Jasmine was furious.

Jim was too scared to repeat himself.

I repeated it for him. "To be near Katherine. Is that right, Jim? Near Katherine?"

Jim nodded and broke down crying.

"The man felt good being in the dark, near Katherine," I continued. "He must have been momentarily spellbound. He must not have known what he was doing. He did not turn on the light, because he felt good staying in the dark. Logic betrayed him. His soul ran ahead of him. He was a shell, his heart had fled . . . What's so incomprehensible about that?"

The crowd stared at Jim with their mouths half-open. Their eyes showed pity. Who would not feel good being in the dark near a goddess?

"But you are a married man," Jasmine said. "According to

Chinese law, adultery is a crime no matter what the circumstances."

"I swear I did not do that," Jim begged. "Besides, it was impossible. She was drunk. Go and take a look at her. Even if I meant to do it, she was in no condition herself."

Jasmine laughed coldly. "How are we to know whether you are telling the truth? The rule is, if you can't prove it, we can only assume. The fact is, I caught you in her room." She raised Jim's slipper in the air. "This is the proof. And everyone here is a witness."

Jim was escorted to Mr. Han's office to be interrogated. Jasmine's version of the event was accepted as truth. Katherine was now a man stealer, a corrupt bourgeois character. She was ruined in Chinese eyes.

I stood before the crowd. "I believe that Katherine didn't do anything with Jim." Turning to Jasmine, I said, "This is not fair to the foreign devil. She's drunk. She cannot defend herself."

"So what are you going to do? Speak for her and prove her innocent?" Jasmine laughed.

"We must have evidence to prove she is guilty," I insisted.

"I have the evidence." Jasmine said each word emphatically.

"No. I'm talking about evidence of actual physical contact."

"We don't need that."

"Yes, we do. You must support your accusation. Katherine is not a Chinese."

The crowd mumbled. People began to argue among themselves. Finally Big Lee suggested that I, as chairman of the Workers' Union, take Jim and Katherine to a nearby hospital to have a doctor do a test to see if the two had intercourse.

The crowd mumbled in agreement. I could see they felt good about having the power to determine the fate of another.

Jasmine thought for a while, then agreed. "If the doctor finds Jim's sperm in her, Katherine will have no way to explain herself. Go do your duty, Comrade Chairman of the Workers' Union."

I walked into Katherine's room. She was sitting on her bed. I asked her how she was doing. She said she still had a headache. The aspirins were not helping. I asked her if she knew what was happening. She said it was too ridiculous for her to care. She told me I looked funny because I was so serious.

I said we had to go outside to take a little walk.

"What for?"

I told her it was very important. Katherine said she didn't feel like going out.

"We're going. I'm taking you to the hospital."

"Why?" she shouted. "There's nothing wrong with me. I just had too much to drink, that's all."

I pulled her off the bed. "You must come with me. You must have a test to prove you are innocent."

"What's going on? Who is behind all this?"

"Remember, you are in China."

Katherine refused to go; she said she looked awful. She was weak. I insisted, and finally she agreed to go but asked me for a few minutes to wash her face.

Jim was ready to go. Katherine finished combing her hair and we left. Jim and Katherine walked two steps ahead of me and the two security guards Jasmine sent along. The crowd parted to make way for us and watched us walk through the front door.

The road to the hospital was filled with garbage left from the morning market. It was only eight o'clock, but the food was all gone. Late shoppers wandered through the market with empty bamboo baskets.

Jim's shame was so heavy his head hung in front of his chest. Katherine walked like a drunken sailor. I caught up to her and took her arm.

It felt ridiculous but it was a serious matter. I hated myself for being one of the Chinese crowd. I was ashamed of this land that produced evil personalities. Katherine asked what I was thinking, and I told her. I didn't care if the guards heard me; I was too angry.

Katherine told me to stop it. She said she didn't like to hear me say such things about China. She criticized me for being narrow-minded and untrusting.

"You can afford to be open-minded and trusting because you don't live here."

"But I do and I'm in trouble. Big Chinese trouble," she said.

I laughed and the sound reminded me of Jasmine's laugh.

Katherine asked me to tell her how this whole thing had started. There would be justice, she said.

"You're about to have a test to see whether you had intercourse with a married man. Isn't that a wonderful kind of justice?"

Katherine went silent. She shook her head.

We entered the hospital and I showed my work pass to a guard at the gate. Seeing that Katherine was a foreigner, he took us straight to the president's office. He asked us to wait and went upstairs. The president came down in a white doctor's gown. He was a tall, slim man and looked kind. I introduced myself and told him why we were there. He listened to me without expression. He gestured for us to sit down and politely asked Jim, "Did you use a condom?" while putting on rubber gloves.

Jim shook his head and said, "I didn't do it."

"Follow me, please," the president said, taking Jim and Katherine to examination rooms.

I sat outside on the bench. My mind was numb.

The test came out negative. I held the hospital record and felt relief. Jim straightened his back and was a new person.

When Jasmine finished reading the record, she said she had things to do and left without another word.

Katherine rolled her eyes toward the ceiling and said she couldn't believe what we did when she was drunk. She said she refused to remember what happened.

Jasmine reported the case to the school Party committee. The Party's conclusion: If there was no wind, there would be no waves. The Party ordered Jim and Katherine to be careful, and to learn a useful lesson from the experience.

Little Bird told me that Jasmine was considering naming me as a reactionary. It didn't surprise me. Jasmine was angry that I got Katherine off the hook. She had already criticized me in a public meeting. She hinted that I had misused my position as the chairman of the Workers' Union to cover up wrongdoing.

I didn't fight back because it was so close to graduation. Jasmine had power over everyone's future. Her father could assign me to hell. My last hope was that the graduation committee would believe that I had acted responsibly instead of out of affection for the foreign devil.

I knew the chance of this was small. The committee might not even bother to confront me with their suspicions. No one would risk offending the Hans to defend me. Mr. Han could punish me without looking like he was giving expression to a personal grudge. This had always been the Party's way.

Every moment I waited for the bomb to drop, and at last it did. My name was called at the graduation ceremony: I was reassigned to Elephant Fields, a wasteland.

There was no explanation. Mr. Han simply said it served the needs of the revolution. I took the assignment letter from him.

I didn't allow myself to break down. I didn't go home to tell my parents the bad news. I took the letter to Katherine. She had been instructed to move back to her hut. She had not been allowed to attend any of the meetings in which her students' fates were decided.

Katherine was not in her hut. One of her neighbors, a local villager, said that she had gone to visit her daughter Little Rabbit at the orphanage.

I waited for Katherine anxiously. I didn't know why I even waited. What could she do? In China the Party's call was law. If I refused to go, I would be deported from my house to Elephant Fields. I tried not to picture Elephant Fields, but it was impossible. I left for home.

Jasmine was assigned to be a translator for a newly appointed army major. Lion Head was offered a teaching position at the school. Jim was to become a middle-school English teacher. Big Lee and Little Lee were to work for the army's new technology department. Little Bird was to be a travel guide. Mr. Han was at his best when it came to punishment. He would make sure his victim was taken out with a clean shot.

My parents sighed when they learned the news at the dinner table. My brother didn't say anything either. The family sat like pieces of stone until the food grew cold. The radio my neighbor kept on all day was playing an old opera song.

> When I was young I said I was sad
> Because I needed the inspiration to write a poem.
> Now I am old
> And have experienced too much sadness.
> When my heart wants to express its feelings
> I say, "Stop it, please stop it . . ."

My mother put down her chopsticks and began to sob silently. She got up and left the table. My father took out a bottle of liquor from under his bed. My brother got two cups from the kitchen cabinet and poured my father and himself drinks. I sat in my chair and felt nothing.

Katherine called me up when she got back and learned of my assignment. I went to her hut and she opened her arms to embrace me when she saw me approach. As she looked at me, tears came to her eyes. She went to pour me tea.

I couldn't think. My nerves were paralyzed. She set the teacup in front of me and went to sit on her bed, placing her head in her palms.

"How's Little Rabbit?" I asked.

"She's fine. We're ready to go, just two more weeks of waiting and she'll be mine."

"Is she . . ."

"Let's talk about you." Katherine got up. "I'm going to get Lion Head here. I have a feeling he might be able to help."

I shook my head and said that Lion Head was a Buddha made of mud—when crossing a river, he had his own life to worry about. "He won't talk to Mr. Han for me. At this point, he wouldn't do a thing to displease Jasmine."

"Give me a chance. Don't you understand? We have nothing to lose now," she said. "I just saw him at the library before I got back here. Let me go get him."

I told Katherine that Lion Head wouldn't be comfortable with me being present, so she suggested I hide in her bed, behind a curtain, when he came.

"Take a nap," she said. "Let the curtain down. Remember to take your shoes in."

Katherine took off on her bicycle in a navy blue wool sweater and black jeans. She rode like a young horse, full of energy and hope.

Katherine's bed smelled like an exotic fragrance. Her blankets were very clean, neatly folded. I wrapped my shoes in my jacket and laid them down carefully in the corner. I was tired. Her pillow was soft. When I moved it, a book fell out. It was *The Good Earth*. I tried to read. Before I hit page 2, I fell asleep.

I heard voices, whispers of a man and a woman.

"I know Zebra needs help but I need help too," the man said. "I need to go to America. I don't want to stay in China and be chewed up by that bitch." It was Lion Head's voice. I woke up but dared not move. Through the curtain I could see Katherine sitting by the table and Lion Head standing very close to her.

Katherine asked if there was no way he could talk to Mr. Han about reassigning me to a better place. "I'll do anything I possibly can to help you in exchange for this favor," she said.

Lion Head pulled up a chair and sat down next to Katherine. He reached out his hand, and, grabbing Katherine's in his own, said, "Marry me, and I'll help Zebra. I am sure I can help her."

There was a long silence. Katherine did not seem to understand.

Lion Head repeated himself.

Katherine said, "Look, this is not a good time for jokes."

Lion Head said he was not joking.

"Why are you making a fool of yourself?" she asked.

"I must secure my own survival first, then I can think about what I can do for you," he replied.

I saw Lion Head's real personality emerge. He was a Zen hypocrite. He had become the master of his own wisdom. He told Katherine that the perfection of Zen was simply to be human and live for one's own needs.

"What are you talking about?" Katherine said.

Rubbing the corner of the table with his index finger, Lion Head said that he didn't expect Katherine to make the sudden leap from common consciousness to "complete, unexcelled awakening." One seeks and seeks, but cannot find. Then one gives up, and the answer comes by itself. Chinese philosophy encourages the intuitive approach in every pursuit, be it remembering a forgotten name or comprehending the deepest principles of Buddhism. Lion Head had now reached the point of pure clarity in his life. He had been thinking about going to the West for a long time. China was a market of butchers and meat. If one did not learn to be a butcher, one would end up chopped meat. This was the life of an average Chinese. And he, Lion Head, was not an average Chinese. He was born to live a freer life. No one could stop him. He would make it one way or another.

Lion Head claimed that he had been used by the Party and now he was learning to use the Party. He needed a fake marriage to get out of the country. If Katherine agreed to marry him, he would do what he could to meet her needs. He didn't have to worry about Jasmine and Mr. Han getting upset, since his assignment had already been made—it would be too late for Mr. Han to change things even if he became suspicious of Lion Head's motives. Once Lion Head accomplished his mission, he would slash Mr. Han's face by telling him that he was going to marry another woman instead of his daughter. If Katherine refused to marry him, well, there was nothing he could do for her.

Katherine was shocked and confused. She was having a hard time convincing herself that Lion Head was not who she thought he was. Her American mind wrestled with her Chinese mind. After a long while, her voice choking a little, she said, "No deal, is that what you're saying? No deal if I refuse to marry you?"

"Come on, Katherine." Lion Head smiled slickly. "Don't force me to disappoint you. After all, it's just a fake marriage I'm asking from you. Just paperwork to get me out of the country. Nothing serious. We each get what we want. Nobody gets hurt."

"You are asking too much and you know it," she said.

"It's not such a terrible thing, considering," he said. "You're in love with China. You and I even have a little history—don't say it wasn't fun. I adored you. I still do. It won't cost you anything to marry me. The minute I set foot in America, we file for divorce. You wouldn't be bothered for very long. You get your deal while I get mine."

Katherine stood up and said in a plain voice: "I don't use people and I don't like to be used. I didn't realize how well you'd learned to manipulate Chinese philosophy. In the spirit of open revolt against convention, you exploit Zen for your own destructive purposes. You, your ego, has become your moral center of gravity—it has nothing to do with the 'spontaneous mind.' You're all about control . . ." Katherine stopped to catch her breath.

I sat behind the curtain, amazed.

Lion Head was amazed by her too, but he tried not to show it. "Katherine, I'm just telling you the naked truth. I'm being honest. I don't dress myself up as a saint to fool you easily. I just want to make an honest deal with you."

Katherine raised her arm and pointed to the door. "There is no deal. Get out, please."

Lion Head got up and walked to the door. Then he turned around. "Katherine, please reconsider my proposal. Forget about the Chinese philosophy."

Katherine shook her head.

"Don't turn me into a mad dog," he said.

Katherine remained silent.

Lion Head said that she was forcing him to take dangerous alternatives.

"What do you mean?" Katherine asked.

The school authority would be selecting one person to study abroad on a United Nations scholarship, he said. The sons and daughters of high Party officials were competing for the position. Mr. Han would make the final decision. Merit was not important. Whoever pleased him most would win. His daughter's happiness was foremost in his heart. But Mr. Han could not choose Jasmine to go abroad because it would look too obvious; he was supposed to be the people's servant, after all. So he would use the opportunity to pick someone who would benefit his family in the future.

"The angel of opportunity is about to land on my head," Lion Head explained. "The chief has been hinting to me to prove my loyalty."

Katherine widened her eyes.

Wearing a sad expression, Lion Head continued: "I have no

choice if you don't help me. I will have to get down on my knees in front of them. I will breathe in their farts and say it smells wonderful. Jasmine is a spoiled brat. She's suffered a great deal of pain and humiliation in trying to get me to be her mate. But I believe her endurance is limited. She expects me to make a decision. If you don't marry me, my only choice is to say yes to Jasmine." He looked off at the rice paddies in the distance. "I'll do anything to get out of this country, anything."

"And then what? You'll desert Jasmine?" asked Katherine.

Lion Head nodded.

"You really are selling yourself," she said. "I am totally amazed. I guess the words 'love' and 'compassion' don't exist in your dictionary."

"Not anymore," said Lion Head. "Once I sold my blood to get back to the city from the countryside. Now I'm selling my soul to have a life. What's the difference? I will have a new life when I get to America. For that dream I am willing to sacrifice everything."

"You think about it," Katherine said slowly. "Zebra is your friend too."

"Only if you marry me . . ." was Lion Head's reply.

"Forget it. I'll talk to Mr. Han myself," Katherine said, her body trembling. "I'll make him change his mind."

Lion Head laughed coldly. "Go and learn your lesson. Get a real taste of the proletarian dictatorship. I wish you good luck!"

I told Katherine not to be foolish. She refused to listen. She said even if Mr. Han were a god, she could still talk to him.

"I'm just going to ask him to be reasonable," she said.

I shook my head. "Your American way doesn't work here."

"It's not the American way. It's the human way. It should apply anywhere," she said.

"Mr. Han doesn't like you, can't you see?"

"Why not? I'm not that important. He has no reason to dislike me."

"Because of your influence over us. You have interfered with his power. Because of you we began to see ourselves as individuals. We began to realize that we didn't need the Party to think for us. We could make decisions for ourselves. We began to question who this man who claimed to be the people's servant really was. You endangered his empire. How could he not hate your guts?"

"But it's your life that's in danger, don't you see?"

"My fate is unchangeable."

"Never, never say that. I'm going to help you change it." Katherine got down on her knees before me. She opened her arms to hug me. "Give it a shot, Zebra. It's your future we're fighting for. You must not give up."

I rested my head on her shoulder and allowed myself to absorb her strength. I heard her heart pounding.

"What about you?" I said.

She lifted my chin to look at me.

"What about me?" she asked.

"If Mr. Han wants, he can label you a 'troublemaker' and kick you out of China."

"He might do that. I can't stop him." Katherine nodded.

"I can't let you risk your future—getting Little Rabbit and finishing your book."

Katherine got off her knees and sat beside me. Taking my hand, she explained that her book was about the lives of Chinese women. By getting involved with my life, she would gain a true understanding of her subject. "And don't worry about Little Rabbit. The adoption is a done deal. The orphanage issues me the official certificate within a week. There is nothing Mr. Han can do to harm me. After I get my daughter, I'll decide whether to stay here or go home."

I slept in Katherine's hut that night. We talked until midnight. Katherine asked if I felt afraid. I said I did because Mr. Han was like the Ru-Lai Buddha who could make his hand grow as big as he wanted. He could cover my universe with his hand, and I was just a foolish monkey who thought his seven hundred thousand cartwheels had gotten him beyond the Buddha's control, only to learn that the column he was urinating on was the Buddha's index finger.

Katherine said that she had never felt so frustrated in her entire life. "Tonight I feel Chinese, truly Chinese."

The next day Katherine went to the chief's office. When she asked to see Mr. Han, she was rejected. The rat-faced secretary told her the chief was not in and was not accepting appointments. "His schedule is fully booked for the month."

A few days later she tried again. This time I went with her. I had never gone to a Party secretary's office without being called first.

"Still too busy to see you," said the secretary.

"That's okay. We'll wait," Katherine said, and took a seat outside the door.

The secretary opened the door and slipped inside the chief's office. Before the door closed again, we saw a tailor measuring the length of Mr. Han's arm. We could overhear their conversation.

"How did it get in your belly?" asked the tailor.

"I don't know," Mr. Han replied. "I was eating a pork chop and it must have fallen out and slid down my throat."

"Did it hurt?"

"No, not at all."

"Then how did you know it was missing?"

"Well, after lunch I realized it was gone! I checked everywhere, I even had people look through the garbage. Not a ghost to be found. Then they told me if I swallowed it I'd better go see a doctor because gold can be very dangerous, maybe even fatal."

"So you went for an X-ray?"

"You bet."

"And? Was it there?"

"You bet. Right there by the belly button. I saw the picture myself. Damn it, it scared the shit out of me."

"Where is it now? Is it out yet?"

"No, it disappeared! Damn it, like a spaceship. Radar isn't good enough to find that thing."

"Have you been checking your shit? Maybe it's already out. Maybe you flushed it down the toilet. Wouldn't that be a pity? It's real gold, eh?"

"I've been checking my shit. In fact, I don't shit in public rest rooms anymore . . . What?!"

We could hear the murmur of the rat-faced secretary.

"Bring her in," Mr. Han said.

The secretary opened the door to the office and waved us inside.

"What's the matter, Miss Katherine?" Mr. Han asked in a warm tone.

Katherine stepped forward and said she would not waste Mr. Han's precious time, she only had one question.

Mr. Han looked at us and told us to sit down. He said that although he was terribly busy he would try to answer her question.

"Why did you reassign Zebra to Elephant Fields? You know there is no need of her skills there."

Mr. Han turned around slowly so the tailor could measure his other arm. He was being fitted for a western suit. "Is that all you have to ask me?"

"Yes."

"This should not be a question," Mr. Han said. "As a Chinese, Zebra understands what it means to listen to the Party's call. You do understand, don't you?" He turned to me. His smile was chilly.

I found myself unable to speak.

"Besides," Mr. Han continued, "it was not my decision alone. It's the Party committee's decision. You see? It is our tradition that individual need yields to the need of the group."

"But, Chief," Katherine said in a gentle voice. "You and I both know what we're talking about here. You are the person in charge. Zebra's future is in your hands. We both know that your daughter doesn't like Zebra and doesn't like the fact that she's friends with me, and that's all right. But as a leader you are expected to play fair. Sending Zebra to Elephant Fields is not fair."

Mr. Han's eyebrows knotted. He flicked off the tailor with his fingers and turned to face Katherine. He smiled strangely and said slowly, "I can forgive you, Miss Katherine, if you make a fool of yourself, because you are an American, but I will not forgive you if you are here to cause student unrest."

"You're right—I am an American, but I'm a human being first," Katherine protested. "I am involved in this case. I don't like seeing my student punished just because she did something to protect me."

Mr. Han expelled a long laugh. Katherine, the tailor, and I stood like walls. The laughter stopped suddenly and Mr. Han said: "You have been brainwashed by the western propaganda machine. You have such a misconception of what I do as Party secretary. I am Jasmine's father, but don't forget that I am the people's servant first. In assigning Zebra to Elephant Fields, there were no personal feelings involved at all. She has to go there because her country needs her."

Katherine tried to stay composed. Taking a breath, she said, "Mr. Han, would you mind if I made our conversation today public?"

"Miss Katherine, I was good enough to make time for your unannounced visit today. Now it sounds as though you are threatening me, and with what, I don't quite understand."

"I can drop the matter entirely if you withdraw Zebra's assignment. If not, I'm afraid I will have to bring it up with the western press and the American diplomatic community."

Mr. Han raised his left arm again and the tailor approached with a sleeve made of muslin. He started to pin the fabric along the length of Mr. Han's arm.

Mr. Han closed his eyes, his chin tilted up.

Katherine glanced at me secretly.

The tailor bent to work on Mr. Han's pants.

A smile came back to Mr. Han's face as he reopened his eyes. He said, "The Party welcomes your criticism any time, Miss Katherine. It is my job to work for you."

"Does that mean you'll withdraw Zebra's assignment?" Katherine wouldn't release her grip.

Mr. Han cleared his throat. Taking out a handkerchief, he blew his nose and laughed again. "I will see if the graduation committee will review the situation."

"When will we know the result?" asked Katherine.

"As soon as we come to one."

"When might that be?"

"You have been in China long enough to know one can't drink hot tea in a hurry."

"I just want your word."

"Let's say two weeks from now."

"To withdraw Zebra's assignment from Elephant Fields, right?"

"Ouch!" Mr. Han kicked the tailor angrily for pricking him with a pin.

The tailor apologized repeatedly.

"May I count on your words, Chief?" Katherine asked.

"You will hear from me two weeks from today."

I smelled evil in the air. I told Katherine so on our way out of Mr. Han's office. Katherine made jokes about my nervousness. I insisted she pay attention to the coming danger. She said living in constant fear was a Chinese illness. Mr. Han had a vicious beam in his eyes when he said his last words, I told her. Katherine laughed and threw a Chinese saying back at me: "Once one was bitten by a snake, for ten years one would be afraid of ropes."

On Sunday, to take my mind off things, Katherine suggested that we go to the orphanage to take Little Rabbit out for a picnic. We got on the train. For the next four hours I listened to American songs on Katherine's Walkman, trying not to think. Katherine read *The Good Earth.*

Little Rabbit opened her arms when she saw Katherine coming. The two screamed happily at each other. Little Rabbit had begun to make sounds and actually talk a little bit. Katherine was obsessed with the idea of making Little Rabbit talk.

Katherine murmured to Little Rabbit that all her papers were ready and she would be allowed to leave the orphanage very soon. Little Rabbit did not understand what Katherine was saying; she was just terribly excited about seeing Katherine. She curled herself in Katherine's arms and buried her head in her chest. She started to call Katherine Mama. Katherine picked up Little Rabbit and the two of them waltzed. Katherine was in tears.

We had dinner at a noodle shop. After dinner Katherine and I took Little Rabbit back to the orphanage. Little Rabbit was promised that she would be picked up in a few days for good.

When Katherine and I got back to the city and said good night to each other, it was already eleven. The night was filled with the sound of wind. It reminded me of a phrase in an ancient poem: "Before the mountain storm arrives, the wind blows its dragon breath through the windows of a tower."

Back at the dormitory, I still felt cold even after I put on all the blankets. It was dawn when I finally drifted into sleep.

Jim woke me. He looked like a mental patient when I opened the door to receive him. His clothes were mismatched. He asked if he could have a quick talk with me out in the hall. I put on some clothes and stepped outside.

Light was just beginning to brighten the hallway. I asked what was the matter.

"There is . . . a typhoon coming!" he said.

I looked out a window onto the quiet campus. "What typhoon?"

"No, not like this. It's . . ." Using gestures, he made me understand that the government had instructed the police to make a mass arrest of suspected criminals.

It was the usual way the Party demonstrated its power.

"Why are you so nervous about that?" I asked.

Jim looked around to make sure no one was there listening. Then he told me. Katherine was on the government's list to be arrested.

I was convinced Mr. Han had plotted the whole thing. He wanted to see Katherine thrown out of China.

I asked Jim how he knew about the list. He said he had a friend who worked for police intelligence. Jim used to confide his fascination with Katherine to him. I asked why he risked his life to reveal a government secret to me.

"I'm still crazy about that foreign devil," he said. "And I feel guilty about the trouble I caused her. I did this for myself."

"What time are they making the arrests?" I asked.

Jim said he was not sure.

I asked Jim if I had his permission to tell Katherine to run off.

"You will do that without my yes or no, I believe." He stared at me and said in a calm voice, "But you and I did not see each other this morning. When you see her though, please shake her hand for me. Tell her I salute her."

I got on my bike and rode as fast as I could to Katherine's hut. Twenty minutes later I was there. A crowd of people stood in front of the hut. I had never seen so many people in these parts. Everyone was quiet. I couldn't tell who were undercover police. I laid my bike on the side of the road and made my way toward the hut. People in front of me blocked my way. They didn't turn their heads when I said excuse me. They had their hands locked together like chains. More people were coming up the road. Among them were some of my schoolmates. News of the arrest had already spread.

I pushed forward, hard. I broke through the human barricade and looked through Katherine's window. In the strange light I could see Katherine standing before two men in police uniforms. They were speaking to her, but she made no response. She must not have known what to say.

One of the men in uniform took out a badge. Waving it in front of Katherine's eyes, he announced himself a police inspector.

The other officer searched her body.

The inspector took out a piece of paper and began to read a

list of charges loudly. The officer took out a pair of handcuffs. Katherine struggled but the two men grabbed her arms and locked them up. She was escorted out of her hut. The crowd engulfed them.

"What have I done?" Katherine shouted.

"You have violated Chinese law," replied the inspector.

I tried to move in closer. Katherine turned her head away the moment she saw me. "Make a report to the U.S. consulate!" she cried.

I understood. I watched as she was put into the black police car parked down the path.

I saw Jim hiding among the crowd. He pretended not to see me.

When the police car drove away, the local police began to search the hut. The crowd grew feverish. They were curious about what the police would find inside.

Fifteen minutes later the police sealed the hut and took off. The gossip began. The foreign devil must have done something awful to have deserved such treatment. Few faces showed sympathy.

I wanted to go straight to the U.S. consulate but knew the minute I touched the gate I would be arrested as a traitor. I would be accused of trying to sell China's secret information. This was not uncommon.

I went to my parents' home and shut myself in the bathroom. I spent two hours writing a letter with my left hand. I described Katherine's arrest and asked that whoever received this letter pass it on to the U.S. consulate.

I went to the Garden Hotel and looked for foreign travelers who spoke with an American accent. Finally I picked out a middle-aged woman who looked kindhearted and followed her. She left the hotel and waved for a taxi. I went up to her and said only, "Please help an American friend." I handed her the letter. She got in a taxi and I followed her on my bike. She got off at the U.S. consulate.

Everyone was talking about the arrest of the foreign devil at school. The news was cooked in a pot of sticky rice—what was true and what was false was indistinguishable and no longer mattered. Arresting Katherine was the government's way of taping our mouths shut. Yet they had to realize that beating heads was the last way to tame minds. Benevolence was always the first choice of rule for our ancient emperors. The goal was to make people obey with their hearts instead of with their mouths.

Twenty-four hours later a mass rally was called. An announcement went out over the public address system. As I walked toward the rally, my schoolmates converged from separate directions. Feelings of distrust and fear separated us. We walked through the trees like pieces on a chessboard, each in his own square, each thinking of protecting himself while staying alert to potential enemies.

A large table with microphones sat in the center of the hall with rows of benches around it. A huge banner in red and black ink hung from the ceiling. It said SWEEP BOURGEOIS TRASH.

Mr. Han sat at the center of the table. To my surprise, Lion Head was sitting next to him. I wondered what he was doing there. He didn't look like himself. He looked like he had stayed up all night. He was biting his nails. His shoulders were stiff when he bent his head to drink tea. Jasmine was sitting off to the right, making scratches in her notebook with a ballpoint pen. She looked confident and charged with energy. She kept looking at the door, watching the people pour in. Jim came in and sat down far off in a corner. He was wearing a green army cap pulled down over his eyes.

The rally began at ten o'clock. All seats were filled.

Katherine entered the hall with two uniformed guards. One guard politely guided her to an empty seat next to Mr. Han. Katherine sat down with grace. She was wearing her dark blue sweater and jeans. Her hair looked like it had just been washed and dried. Although she wore no makeup, her lips appeared red in contrast to her pale skin. I looked at her and felt my deep worship of her beauty and character. She still looked trusting.

I was nervous. I sat way in the back, far from Katherine but in her line of sight. Next to me were Big Lee, Little Lee, and Little Bird. I wanted nobody to be able to detect my emotions. I covered myself with an old green army jacket. I had the chills. I watched Jasmine. I could detect her hidden grin. I could tell she took pleasure in this event. She had become the operator of her father's torture chamber.

Katherine did not look nervous. She looked as if she were ready for a show to begin. Her clear eyes mirrored her guiltless heart.

But she was making a big mistake. She forgot she was in China. She was a newborn ox who did not know the tiger was an enemy. She did not know the tiger's bite would be fatal.

Mr. Han stood up and opened the meeting by saying that the Party committee had something to reveal and sought the masses' opinion. He moved the microphone closer to Lion Head.

Lion Head took out a blue cotton bag and laid it on the table. He took some sheets of paper out of the bag. His hands were trembling. His face turned red, blue, then gray. Sweat gathered on the tip of his nose. Finally he took out a magazine. On the cover was a nearly naked western woman. Across the top was the word *Playboy.*

I could feel my blood gush up to my forehead. I recognized the name of the magazine. One could be arrested and jailed for reading such a magazine.

Katherine must have felt like eating worms when she saw Lion Head take out the *Playboy* magazine from his bag. She must have thought Lion Head was joking with her at the wrong time. She stared at him and her face swelled.

The second shock came before the first faded away: In the same slow motion, Lion Head took out a handful of photos. They were the nude pictures he had taken after I had painted Katherine's body. My anger rose. I wanted to eat Lion Head up, drink his blood and chew his intestines. I hated myself for having provided him with the opportunity to harm Katherine.

The masses were disturbed. The older people looked at Katherine with disgust in their eyes. The young people watched with interest and secretly gloated over the foreign devil's misfortune. The men stretched their necks long, sucking up the images with their eyes. The women kept their eyes fixed on the pictures, missing no detail. They held their breath and looked hard at those apple breasts and horselike hips. Western glory provoked oriental shame. Sympathy disappeared in the women's eyes. Envy became anger. The masses' minds were bleached with alkali.

Mr. Han and Jasmine sat quietly, taking in the reaction of the masses. They made no comment, not a sound. They let the moment ferment. I remembered how Jasmine once proudly told me about the art of her father's leadership. "It's like holding thunderbolts in your hand," she said. "The trick is to release them one by one."

Mr. Han nodded at Lion Head and asked him to be brief and not graphic. Lion Head bit his lips for a while and made an effort to spit out a few words. Waving the magazine and photos above his head, he said, "I was seduced by her." He pointed his finger at Katherine. "We had an illegal relationship. She performed on me various sexual acts . . ." He stopped. He said no more. He didn't have to.

Mr. Han looked satisfied. He said that was enough. There was no need to be more graphic about the incident. China needed no more "spiritual pollution."

Mr. Han announced that unless Katherine could give the name of an individual who had influenced her to act in this way, her criminal record would be hereby established and she could expect no favor from the Chinese legal system because of her nationality.

They were trying to get Katherine to denounce me.

I looked at Katherine. She looked up at me. We both understood what they wanted. I felt panic; my mind seized up. I didn't know what else Lion Head had told them. I didn't know what I could expect of Katherine. She could be held for interrogation, humiliated. They would use Mao's *zah* technique of painting a larger-than-life picture of horror to scare her into saying what they wanted. She was an American. Could she endure this? How could I know she wouldn't do to me what Lion Head had done to her?

The hall was so quiet I could hear the heavy breath of the crowd. A dry cough from the corner vibrated in the air.

Katherine smiled, to herself first, then at me, then at the

room. The strength of her smile lifted my spirit. I believed that her will was unbreakable.

Mr. Han cleared his throat. "You do not have to go through this, you know. You are our guest, Miss Katherine. We can suppose you loaned the magazine with no evil intention, you posed for pictures in innocence, not knowing you were being used. But you must tell us who was behind this. We believe there was another influence, somebody who pretended to be your friend. Give us the name."

"There is no such name, I'm sorry," said Katherine.

"Would you like to complete your project on Chinese women?" asked Mr. Han.

"I don't see how this has anything to do with my research," said Katherine.

"It will have a big effect on your research," said Mr. Han. "To the Chinese, morality is everything. We will accept no one who causes our moral values to deteriorate. We will allow no bad influence to poison the minds of our young people."

"This is a setup," said Katherine.

"I'm sorry that you have given me no choice." Mr. Han stood up, addressed the masses, and released his final thunderbolts. His voice was loud and clear. "As the representative of the Party committee, I hereby announce that this woman is no longer an employee of our school. She has stained our good name by spreading western pornography and posing for nude photographs which insult our moral tradition. Her research material will be confiscated to prevent her from doing harm to our country in the future. And the orphan . . ."

As if hearing an explosion, Katherine jumped up from her seat.

"Have you changed your mind?" Mr. Han asked.

Slowly shaking her head, Katherine replied, "No." Tears began to gather in her eyes as she sat back down.

Mr. Han announced that the certificate of adoption would be nullified.

Mr. Han ordered Katherine to leave the country within ten days. She was not permitted to enter China again.

Raindrops tapped the leaves. The crowd came out of the hall holding newspapers over their heads. To my people, this event was just one of hundreds they had attended in their lives. At this moment nothing bothered them more than the raindrops. My people had their own lives to worry about. If one could not immediately benefit from Katherine, why should one care?—a common post–Cultural Revolution attitude. It was foolish of her to have come to China in the first place. Anyway, this would not be the end of her life, they told themselves. Once she was back in America she would wake up from the nightmare and be glad she was still alive. So what harm did the chief's announcement actually do her? The child? The child she could live without. An orphan was not meant to live a good life anyway.

I held a newspaper over my head, like everyone else, and felt barely alive.

It was too late when the statement came from the U.S. consulate asserting Katherine's rights as an American. She was released right after the meeting. "No future harm will befall her," the school promised the consulate.

———

Katherine was being taken away from me. How would I bear missing her?

I was unable to take another look at Katherine. Even as she rose from the bench, I had run out of the hall. I would not be able to say goodbye to her. My will shut down from fear. Ten days.

I remembered a long letter my great-uncle wrote our family at the age of seventy-three when he was finally accepted as a member of the Communist Party. He was extremely happy. He said he could now die in peace tomorrow. He said his biggest fault in life was that he did not make himself a relative of the Communist Party in time. It was the root of all his misery. He had suffered enough for his fault; now he made peace with himself.

I did not know how to accept my great-uncle's letter. His letter made me feel very sad. He was like garlic cooked bitter by fear. He no longer tasted like garlic; his individuality was lost. He was transformed by the Party machine. And the saddest thing was that he was happy with the result. Who was he now? Was this the same great-uncle who used to write poems praising the magnificent strength of snow lilies in Tibet? In my eyes he had become a clown who danced to please his master during the holiday season.

It was a sad story, but people who lived sad stories often did not feel the sadness.

Katherine made me feel the sadness I was living through. I would never become my great-uncle. Because I would never let her go.

In the evening I helped Mother make blankets for winter at Elephant Fields. We sat opposite each other on the bed, sewing for hours. Mother immersed herself in the work. Her hands moved slowly but steadily. I tried to concentrate on making the stitches in a straight line, but my fingers betrayed me. I felt a deep anger rise inside me, slashing me to pieces. My heart felt as if it could burst at any time.

I drew in a deep breath. Mother raised her head, looked at me over her thick glasses. She stared at me motionlessly. I exhaled my breath quietly, eyes fixed on the stitches. Mother went back to her needle.

I watched the crooked stitches grow under my hands like the trace of a snail, thinking how much the broken line looked like my life.

Lion Head finally made Jasmine a happy woman. He belonged to her. He stopped talking about Zen. He underwent a sudden and revolutionary change. He had come to a real relationship with the self, a mutuality in which he, the knower, no longer felt himself independent of the known; he no longer stood apart from experience. And experience had become absurd. He said that everything had become vividly clear. In concrete fact he had no self other than the totality of things of which he was aware. He said he had ordered his feelings to retire completely.

Three days after Katherine's fate was determined, Lion Head's name was posted on the campus bulletin board as the comrade selected to go to America to study on the United Nations scholarship. Flowers made of red wrinkled paper encircled his name. His smiling picture stared out at viewers. Underneath the picture a line read: CONGRATULATIONS, COMRADE HEAVENLY LION, THE PRIDE OF OUR GRADUATES!

Lion Head and Jasmine appeared hand in hand on campus. They were engaged. Jasmine could hardly keep herself composed. She attached herself to Lion Head like a leech. She wore a tight red-and-white-checkerboard nylon shirt and an above-the-knee green skirt. A pair of modern-looking brown plastic shoes. It was a sunny day and she had her black cotton umbrella up. The couple showed themselves off around campus. Jasmine would occasionally lower the umbrella so she could glue her head to his.

I didn't know what was on Lion Head's mind. I didn't care to know. I was certain Jasmine was living an illusion of love. Lion Head had accomplished his goal. I did not feel sorry for Jasmine. She and Lion Head deserved each other.

I went with my father to visit a ninety-year-old great-aunt. He said it could be our last chance before she passed away.

My great-aunt lived on the top floor of a four-story house. The staircase was narrow and as dark as a cave. We kept tripping over our own steps. My great-aunt had a small room off a sunny porch. She was such a feverish flower lover, she had made the porch into a garden. I used to come here to see the flowers bloom, but now I saw no flowers. The clay pots were either broken or laid sadly empty on the concrete. The bamboo trellises slanted off the brick wall. A couple of dry leaves of ivy dangled in the wind.

Aunt Golden Moon and Aunt Silver Moon, my great-aunt's daughters, greeted us at the door. "Be sure to speak loudly," my father said to me as he bowed to his cousins.

"It doesn't matter anymore," Aunt Silver Moon said. "Mother can hardly hear or see."

I didn't see my great-aunt in the room. I asked where she was. Aunt Golden Moon pointed at a pile of blankets. I turned my head and was shocked to see my great-aunt had shrunk to the size of a small child.

I asked how Great-Aunt spent her days, whether she knew that death was approaching. Was she afraid? Had she had enough of the world? Did she talk about life after death? My father told me to stop asking such "*bu-ji-li*" questions that would bring bad luck, but I couldn't help myself.

Aunt Silver Moon smiled and said that it seemed like Great-Aunt was having fun. She stayed in bed all the time. "Just like an infant," she said. "She plays in bed, mumbling words and singing songs from her childhood. She pees and shits in diapers and hates to be washed."

"Come and see what she's playing now," Aunt Golden Moon said, and she pulled over a chair. She sat me by the bed.

"Great-Aunt!" I called. No response. Aunt Golden Moon pulled the curtains aside. The light seemed to wake the little creature. She curled like a worm. The two daughters went to cuddle their mother, and she giggled with her eyes closed and her clawlike little hands waving in the air. My father propped Great-Aunt up with several pillows. Aunt Silver Moon passed her mother a box of candies.

Great-Aunt picked up a piece of candy and gave it to me. Before I could open the wrapper, Aunt Golden Moon came and took the candy away. She whispered to me that Great-Aunt had already opened and licked each candy. "It's her toy," she said. "She opens one, tastes it, and wraps it back up. Over and over again. She loves to explore things, just like a child. She doesn't let anyone touch the box. It's the only thing she remembers to ask for when she wakes up."

I sat by the living mummy while my father and his cousins went in the kitchen. I watched Great-Aunt suck each candy and throw it back in the box. What did living mean to this creature? I envied Great-Aunt's brainlessness. She had no worries, no despair. A life without pain. Such a way of leaving the world seemed to be the kindest thing God in heaven could grant a person.

Leaves began to drop from the tree of my spirit. I could only lie in torment. I could only let the dead leaves brush my stone-cold face. In the far reaches of my mind the leaves sang sad songs as they were swept away by the bitter wind.

It was two days before Katherine's departure. In the afternoon I received a letter from her. When the mailman handed me the letter, my hands trembled.

Inside was a card made of straw paper with a poem written in black ink.

> *You came unprotected like a bud in winter*
> *On a willow tree, eager to take on nature's plan.*
> *Did you realize the struggle?*
> *Were you aware of the forces that*
> *Tried to keep you down?*
>
> *Despite all inclement fury*
> *A beautiful sculpturesque*
> *Branch you became, welcoming*
> *The breeze and accepting*
> *The frost.*
>
> *My Goddess in armor*
> *I love you.*

In her P.S. she asked me to meet her on her last afternoon in China. She said that besides saying goodbye she needed a favor from me and would let me know what it was when we met.

The address she had given me was a brick façade located next to a smelly food market on the south side of the city. Behind the façade, ramshackle apartment houses rose on either side. The alley was dark. The air smelled like hen shit. I heard babies crying. The sound of someone scrubbing a chamberpot. As I made my way through the passageway, I bumped my head on an aluminum pot that hung overhead. Wet towels brushed my face. I almost stumbled over a smoking stove. The long, deep cough of an old lady came from the opposite window. After the cough came the old lady's cursing: "You are tightening the strap on a hanging ghost! No need to, you hear me?" Kids' screaming came from streets. A mother was spanking her child. She called him a preserved cucumber and threatened to break him in two. A flying broom crossed my path. The child ran by and shot down a narrow staircase.

I came to the courtyard and ran into the mother who was chasing her boy.

"Who are you?" she asked me, irritated.

"I am looking for room number nine."

The woman pointed her finger up high and said that it was the attic. She hurried off after the boy.

Before I could knock, the attic door opened a crack, and Katherine's face appeared. She quickly let me in and closed the door behind me.

"Jim lent me this room," Katherine explained. "It was his uncle's room. His uncle died about a month ago and the government hasn't reclaimed the room yet."

There was no light in the room. Daylight came in through broken shutters. There was no furniture. Katherine sat down on the floor. She gestured for me to sit beside her.

"How are you?" she asked.

I nodded. It felt difficult to speak.

"I need your help." She looked anxious.

I nodded again.

"Please help raise Little Rabbit when I'm gone. Here is all the money I have. One thousand U.S. dollars. I'd like you to take over the adoption, use the money to buy off the authorities if necessary. I'll send you more money through Jim. He'll let us use his mailbox. He will change the dollars to Chinese money for you. Will you help me?"

I saw tears glittering in her eyes. I wanted to tell her that I would do anything for her. I took her money and placed it carefully in my inner pocket.

She took my hands and put her head in my palms. Her tears wet my sleeves. I bent to embrace her. Lifting her chin, I looked at this face. I remembered the first day I saw her in class.

She smiled. I asked what time her flight was.

"Early tomorrow morning," she replied. Her voice carried no energy. "I can't believe I'm not allowed to enter China again. You were right, I was too naive about this country."

We went silent. The sunshine slowly moved toward the west. Noises came from the food market below. The afternoon shopping time had begun. People were screaming and yelling to get ahead of each other in line. A vendor swore, calling her customer "Pig Brains." I could hear the sound of tin scales.

What images would Katherine take back with her from China?

"You must tell me about Elephant Fields," said Katherine. "I know it's going to be extremely difficult for you. I'm ashamed that I couldn't help. But I am going to try. In any case, we must, must keep in touch."

I nodded and then asked what time we had to leave this place and whether she would have time to have dinner with me. She said we had to be out in fifteen minutes. She had to go to the library to return all her books before it closed. I realized that this was my last time to be with her.

"Thank you," she said.

"You are welcome," I said, my words stuck.

We didn't know what else to say to each other.

"Thanks for everything you shared with me, I mean everything . . ." She lost her words. She tried to smile. Failed. She sighed and turned away. I looked at her remarkable lynx eyes. She entered my memory moment by moment.

Despair overwhelmed me. I didn't know what would happen to me at Elephant Fields, didn't know who from my wretched past I would find there. I did not know whether I would even be permitted to contact Katherine. I couldn't warn her about it. I could not shut down her hope. Little Rabbit was her baby. I had to keep her hope alive.

Katherine was no longer an American guest. She had lived a Chinese life, not a long one but an intense one. She had learned everything she was supposed to learn about China but one thing: she still did not understand that my spiritual life ended here, right at this moment. I could feel Satan knocking on my heart's door, hurrying me to hell.

"Dance with me," Katherine said as she took a tiny cassette player from her bag. "We'll keep the volume low."

Without waiting for my response, she took me by the hand. She held me tight.

The music was so soft we could hear the floor squeak under

our feet. Our shadows moved on the wall. I leaned my head on her shoulder. She pulled me in, slowly. Her breath hit my cheek. I wanted to tell her that I had been in love with her since the first day I met her. I wanted to tell her that I couldn't imagine life without her.

As if she knew what I was going to say, she wouldn't give me the chance to talk. She held me, her eyes closed. Her hair smelled like fresh flowers. Her fingers came to soothe my face. I closed my eyes and felt the rhythm of her body.

"I am taking you with me," she murmured. "I am taking you."

I opened my eyes.

I saw tears running down her face.

I held her, trying to feel her, her love, her shape, her voice. My America, farewell.

As a borrowed worker, I was "honorably returned" to Elephant Fields. Mr. Han did not speak with me, not even a word, after graduation. The notice of my departure was posted on the door of my parents' home. It was marked with a deadline date and had an official red Party stamp. I was a skeleton nailed in a coffin. Mr. Han blew me away like dust. My family could do nothing but weep for me.

Mother spent all her savings buying fresh meat and vegetables to feed me as if every meal was my last on earth. She cooked spicy meat and bean paste and put it in jars for me to take along. My father stir-fried bags of flour I could eat with hot water as a kind of porridge. My parents did everything silently, preparing me and themselves for my departure.

My schoolmates and neighbors had nothing to say about my assignment. Indifference was the Chinese way. "Clean up the snow in your own yard, pay no attention to the frost on other people's roofs."

As a last-ditch effort, I wrote Mr. Han and the district Party committee letters demanding to be treated fairly. The letters were like stones thrown in water—I received no response. I felt like a mantis trying to stop a carriage with its legs. I was vanishing,

vanishing into the ocean of a billion people. I became faceless and voiceless.

Bus, train, train, and bus, days and nights, passing mountains and rivers through central China—my journey was a ride to hell. When a tractor finally dropped me off at Elephant Fields, I lost my strength completely. For a while I was not able to get on my feet and walk. My whole being was paralyzed, a chill froze my blood. My pupils enlarged, my vision blurred, my limbs were numb. I lay on my stomach, my breath thinner than thread.

Elephant Fields looked the same, the "ear" standing out like a giant chip against the sky. The vast gray land made me feel small as an ant. I had no tears. Having escaped hell only to be returned made me learn the depth of pain. Slowly I forced myself to stand up and walk.

By evening I was registering at the Party secretary's office, a wooden house that carried the sound of the wind's whistle. The Party boss told me that he had just been appointed to the job. He was a sixty-five-year-old man named Lao Guener—Old Woodstick. His Mao jacket was patched with different-colored cloth. He said he had received my dossier from the Shanghai Party office and he knew who I was. If I didn't have anything more to explain, he would just assign me to a tent with two other female workers. I asked if there were bad things written about me in the dossier so I would know what I had to explain. He said he couldn't possibly tell me, it was against Party law.

"The past is not that important, Chairman Mao once taught us," Lao Guener said, his breath smelling strongly of tobacco. "What's important is how you behave from now on. Everybody's got a pair of eyes. I believe what I see. So my point is don't worry about what's in your dossier."

As he showed me to my tent, I asked him about some of my ex-workmates. Lao Guener told me that with the Central Bureau's policy change of 1980, all city youths were allowed to leave. Overnight, thousands of people packed up and left. The only ones who stayed were local peasants, the city youths who had married locals and had children (their children were not allowed to go to the cities), and ex-criminals who were too ashamed to go home. Elephant Fields had also been used as a rehabilitation camp.

"We've made a lot of progress," Lao Guener said proudly. "Look at this city of tents. It reminds me of my days as a Red Army soldier. This way the revisionists will never be able to corrupt our proletarian spirit."

As I unpacked, the smell of dynamite once again overwhelmed me. My tentmates were local peasants. They were illiterate and spoke a dialect I couldn't understand. We looked at each other like birds. They showed me the nearest path to the pond for water.

I shut down all my senses and worked like a machine. We slept in rows of tents and went to work wherever the job took us. The workers sang, "The sky is my blanket and the rocky ground my bed." I went to work dressed in stars and came back to the tent carrying the moon on my head. After the first week my muscles began to ache. My chest hurt when I coughed or took a shit. The fifty-pound hammer once again became my only companion.

I tried to find traces of the life I had lived here before. The riverbank where I had my miscarriage had dried up. The bushes nearby were gone. Only the sky was the same, gray as a dead person's skin.

We melted ice cubes to cook food. There was no place to shower. My skin flaked like an animal's in the desert. When my body itched, I would rub my back against a wall like a bear.

I made fifty yuan a month and sent twenty-five to a village nanny who had been taking care of Little Rabbit for me. The nanny lived twenty miles away from me.

I'd played tricks to get Little Rabbit out of the orphanage. I figured that after Katherine was gone, Mr. Han couldn't care less about what happened to Little Rabbit. So I faked papers that convinced the headmistress of the orphanage that the case against Katherine had been mishandled and I stuffed her pockets with money.

She said, "No! I cannot take any money from you."

"What about donations?" I asked.

She nodded hesitantly.

"Then consider these two hundred yuan a donation."

Little Rabbit was released to me. I asked the headmistress what had happened to the certificate of adoption that had been prepared for Katherine. She said she didn't know what to do with the document, but wasn't sure she should give it to me. I said I just wanted to keep it, I would not show it to anybody.

"You have a very nice watch," she said.

I took off my watch. "It's yours." Again she didn't want to take it, and again I called it a donation. She took the watch and gave me the certificate.

My life was once again empty. During the day I worked with dynamite. At night I played the tapes Katherine left me on her Walkman. Her poem lay under my pillow. Although I tried to live up to her image of a "goddess in armor," I couldn't delude myself that life could change if only my will stayed strong. I imagined Katherine's life in America. I imagined her in a car and wondered how it felt to ride in a car.

I was attacked by nightmares—the most frightening was one in which Katherine had forgotten us. I woke up thinking, She was a foreigner, after all. She's getting on with her life. Maybe she'd adopted children from other countries or got married and was thinking about having children of her own.

Three months had passed, and it felt like thirty years. In the absence of hope, insanity set in. One day I was boiling water on a gasoline stove outside my tent. The wind suddenly changed direction and the tent caught fire. My tentmates told me I stood still, watching the fire chew up the tent. I was shocked at myself afterward. If my tentmates hadn't been there, I would have let the fire keep burning. I knew I would have. I wouldn't have done a thing.

Little Rabbit was my only link to sanity. She had grown taller and had two pigtails. The village nanny and her family were kind to her. The nanny had been trying to correct bad habits she had developed at the orphanage, like peeing or shitting wherever she happened to be. It amazed me to hear her talk like a normal person with a voice. She was Katherine's miracle. She told me that she wanted to look like Katherine when she grew up.

"I am going to eat a lot so I can have a *pe-gue* as big as my mama's, even bigger," she said seriously, her hands making the shape of buttocks in the air. She had a good imagination too. She would describe to me how a fly was trying to steal the crackers she was eating.

One afternoon as I sat chatting with the nanny, it began to rain outside. Little Rabbit climbed up on a chair and watched rain drip off the window frame. She was quiet for a long time, then all of a sudden, she stretched out her arms toward the sky and said, "Stop crying! Why are you crying? *Nao-mee-bee.*" Shame on you. Then she jumped off the chair and came to sit on my lap. She asked me why the sky was crying. I didn't answer her. I was thinking about Katherine.

After her nap, Little Rabbit was still thinking about the crying sky. She said to me, "When I was sleeping, the rain came to cry in my body. I said, 'No! It's bad to cry.' The rain got mad and made me pee in my bed. *Nao-mee-bee.*"

Katherine was missing so much.

The mailman became the object of my secret obsession. He came once a week on a tractor. When he called out the names on the packages and envelopes he delivered was a time of hope and disappointment. I accumulated countless disappointments, but every week I still had a little hope.

The first day of the fourth month since my arrival, Katherine's first letter arrived. It came through Jim. He sealed her letter in a Chinese envelope and sent it on to me. My heart zigzagged in my chest when I opened the envelope. "It's her writing, her touch," I heard myself murmur. I ran until I exhausted myself. In tears, I lay on my back in the field. I kissed the letter over and over. Katherine, Katherine, Katherine, I called.

She wrote that she had corresponded with Jim the minute she

landed in America to make sure that it would work. At first the letters came back marked "return to sender," but recently the letters got through. She guessed it was because there was more and more business communication between the two countries; it was impossible for the Chinese government to spy on every private letter. She said she was working as an associate professor in the history department of a California college and she was well. She'd told her family and friends about me and Little Rabbit and she believed that we would meet again. She asked how I was doing and said she was missing me and Little Rabbit to pieces.

I tried to write back, but it was a hard letter to compose. What should I write about? My life as a prisoner? The development of my joint problems? How my blisters bled every night? The pain of my dry, peeling skin? How the food tasted like sand and how I peed and shit like a mountain goat on rocks?

I decided to write about Little Rabbit, telling her about the child's dreams and way of talking. I could hear Katherine laughing. How I missed her laugh! I avoided talking about myself because I didn't want to upset her. Katherine would have a good idea of what kind of life I led at Elephant Fields anyway.

I copied the letter onto a clean sheet and placed it beneath my pillow. I wrote Jim's address on the envelope. The next morning before work I went to the local post office. The postal clerk asked me if the letter carried any urgent message because the mail was only collected from this box once a month. The next closest box was six miles away, but the mail was picked up once a week. I ran to the other post office and mailed the letter off.

In her return letter Katherine wrote that she had been screaming for joy for three days. Hearing from me made her feel like she had woken up from a coma. She told me she had been closely studying China's changing role in the world. She wrote that there were over fifty thousand Chinese students in the United States and she was investigating how they had made it over.

"You didn't tell me anything about your life at Elephant Fields," she wrote. "I can figure it out for myself. I can feel your pain just like I can feel your joy. I think of you every day . . ."

I went to work carrying Katherine's letter. The explosions of dynamite sounded exciting. For the first time I enjoyed the grand scene of millions of tiny stones raining down after the blast. Also for the first time I paid attention to Lao Guener's monthly progress report, which said that our division had produced the best rocks for building roads. We'd been named the "model labor team" of Elephant Fields.

I went to visit Little Rabbit one evening and told her that her mother had written. She widened her eyes and all of a sudden threw a temper tantrum. She smashed her rice bowl on the floor and said I was lying to her. Her mother had forgotten to pick her up as she had promised.

I held Little Rabbit tightly. I didn't know what to say.

I wrote to Katherine again and reported Little Rabbit's disappointment.

"Every morning I wake up thinking to myself, I've got to get Little Rabbit out!" she wrote. "No one ever said giving birth was easy. No one is going to keep my child away from me, no one."

Another three months passed. Katherine's latest letter brought great news. She had explained my situation to the president of her school and showed him pictures of my paintings. The school had agreed to admit me to its fine arts program and would offer me a scholarship. "Now it's time to do your part. You must get permission for you and Little Rabbit to leave. Find out how far the long road of bureaucracy stretches and be prepared for how it may confound you. I'm still working on this on my end. Promise me you won't give up."

I hit my head with my fist because I couldn't believe this was real. I looked around. Covered with dust, all the workers looked like white bears. Was this the end of my misery? I lost sleep in my excitement.

I wrote to everyone I knew asking how one got permission to go to America as a student. Jim wrote with information on procedure. Big Lee and Little Lee also answered my letter, giving me tips and encouragement. Little Bird checked with one of her relatives in the city foreign affairs office and sent applications for passports for me and Little Rabbit. I drew up a statement of purpose and presented it to the local Party boss as Jim instructed.

I waited for Lao Guener's response to my letter. Every waking second was spent waiting. A couple of times I lit a stick of dynamite, tossed it, and drifted off in thought until a co-worker would yell at me to run.

Finally, two weeks after I had submitted the letter of intent, Lao Guener called me into his office at lunchtime. I brought along a dirt-colored canvas bag that contained ten cartons of cigarettes I bought with Katherine's money. I would look for any chance to flatter and corrupt him. My legs were trembling. I tried to calm down, tried to look relaxed, tried not to think what would happen if he rejected my request.

Like an owl, Lao Guener squatted on his heels on a narrow wooden bench next to his tree-stump table. Half the table was piled high with Mao's books coated with dust. Lao Guener was drinking tea and smoking a pipe. He looked tired and hadn't bathed for a long time. His facial hair was messy, his Mao jacket greasy. He pointed for me to sit down on another bench.

I bit my lips in nervousness. My mind was boiling. Lao Guener held the same power as Mr. Han had held over my future. Was he in a bad mood this morning? Was he annoyed with me? Did he sleep well last night? Did he reread my dossier? Would he judge me on the basis of the reports Mr. Han had written or would he use his own eyes as he had said? My work at Elephant Fields was invulnerable to criticism—Lao Guener himself had praised me as a good worker—but wouldn't he be selfish about losing a valuable laborer? Were the tobacco leaves in his pipe dry enough to keep burning and soothing his brain? Or was he going to cough and feel irritated?

I felt like a criminal on an execution platform. My life hung on the tip of Lao Guener's tongue. One word from his mouth and my head would either dance on my shoulders or roll on the floor.

Lao Guener cleared his throat and spit flew from his mouth. He said something I could not hear. I only saw his tea-leaf-colored teeth moving. I bit down hard on my lip and concentrated on his thick cracked lips. I heard him ask me to explain what my letter was all about.

I began my long prepared speech. I said going to America to study was a way to requite the Party's kindness. When I came back I would help Communism take a stronger hold in China with the knowledge I'd acquired.

Lao Guener interrupted me impatiently. He asked what

America was. I let out a breath. At least I wouldn't have to explain why I chose to go to such an imperialistic country. I said that America was a nation of people of many different races—and a lot of proletarians. Lao Guener asked where it was located. I replied that it was on the other side of the ocean. He was still unclear.

"Is it near Albania?" he asked.

I thought he must have good feelings about Communist Albania, so my mouth moved. "Not too far from Albania."

"Do you plan to spread revolution in America?" Lao Guener flipped his pipe over and tapped the ashes out on the table.

"Of course. If I get the chance," I said.

"No! As a revolutionary, you must look for chances to spread revolution! You must be active about it!" He became strangely excited. "When I was a young Red Army soldier, I spread revolution wherever I went, village to village, port to port. Nothing stopped me, nothing! Why? Because I was active, aggressive, and determined about it."

I asked if he would release me.

"I don't see why not. I don't see anything wrong with spreading revolution in Albania . . ." he answered.

"America," I reminded him in a small voice.

"Of course, America. It doesn't matter. What matters is we do our best to put red dots all over the map, right?"

"Right," I echoed.

"Now tell me, what do you need?" he asked, filling his pipe with new tobacco.

I asked if he would issue me a letter of release and permit me to take a leave of absence from my work because I needed to collect stamps of approval from different government organizations. He nodded and said he knew how bureaucracy ran rampant through the city.

"To tell you the truth," he said, "I never understood why all the city youth went home and you were sent back."

I told him about Mr. Han. Lao Guener shook his head and said that he understood my situation completely. Half the workers at Elephant Fields who came from the city had been sent for similar reasons.

"During the fifties people with thinking problems were called 'rightists'; in the sixties they were 'counterrevolutionaries'; in the seventies, 'reactionaries.' I wonder, what are they called now in the eighties?" Lao Guener sighed and lit his pipe. "There's just the matter of your educational fee for all you've learned here at Elephant Fields . . ."

I knew this was his indirect way of asking for gifts. I opened my bag and slid it across the table.

He asked me to write the letter for him to sign saying I was a good comrade and that he had no problem releasing me.

Buddha in Heaven, I thank you. Katherine, keep praying for me. At night I lay outside my tent celebrating my first victory. The stars shone clearly, the moon looked so close and the air was chilly. Would I make it through? The wind answered me with its whistle.

The letter proving my good comrade status began to travel along with my application for a passport. It went on to get stamps from the district Party office to the town Party office, to the county Party office, the provincial Party office, and finally the Party's National Educational Bureau. The letter got stuck twice, once for the stated reason that "certain documents are missing," and then because "family background needs to be reinvestigated." I waited patiently and humbly checked every month with the authority. Four months passed. When I checked again, I was told that "the documents have been misplaced and are in the process of being traced." I knew the whole thing must have been lost. I filed the application all over again.

There were days when I grew tired of waiting. I felt my hope ebbing. I feared there was a bigger problem than that "the documents have been misplaced." The Chinese way of punishing a person was never direct.

On a cold November day I got off work, stepped into the tent, dog-tired, and found a dirty envelope on my blanket. I picked it up. The minute I opened it, my breath stopped. I got down on my knees and took out a little brown book with a plastic cover. My passport.

That night I danced with the envelope outside my tent. My co-workers thought I had a ghost in my body performing witch-craft.

Contacting the foreign affairs office in Shanghai was my next task. I was switched to seven different telephone operators and finally reached the party I needed. I was in a town several miles from Elephant Fields. I spent two hours on the road just to make this call. I was told that Little Rabbit's passport was on its way.

I hurried to the nanny's house to pick up Little Rabbit, and to my horror the child was not there. The nanny told me that people from the orphanage had come for her.

My mind went blank. I couldn't figure out what was going on. I rushed to the bus station but the last bus of the night had left. I walked overnight to the orphanage. I arrived at five o'clock in the morning with my clothes wet from dew.

I was told Little Rabbit was being kept in an isolation room. The headmistress said that she was ordered to take Little Rabbit back because the child had been assigned to a Taiwanese family for adoption. Her new parents were on their way.

"Why?" I gasped.

"Why?" she said viciously. "Ask yourself!"

"I don't understand."

She stared straight into my eyes. Pointing her middle finger at the tip of my nose, she said, "You forged the papers, didn't you?"

I silently admitted my crime.

"One reaps what one plants," the headmistress said.

"But Little Rabbit was assigned to Katherine," I insisted.

"How can you say this as if you hadn't lived through the Cultural Revolution at all," she said sarcastically.

"Did you report me?"

"No," she said, bending down to pick up a stack of papers. She threw it on her desk and flipped through the pages. "I was questioned by a secretary from the top. But I covered your ass by saying that I didn't know how the case had gotten so messy. I said someone from my office must have mixed up Little Rabbit's case with someone else's. Anyhow, Little Rabbit has to go, and this time I can't do anything about it."

I paced the orphanage's courtyard back and forth. The head-mistress felt sorry for me since she had taken my donations. I asked if she could put the Taiwanese couple on hold for a couple of days, not knowing if there really was a Taiwanese couple or if the whole thing had been made up as a way of thwarting my plans. She said she didn't have to put the case on hold because a contagious virus called "the #2 disease" was sweeping through the orphanage. The virus caused a high fever that could eventually attack the brain. Most of the children had no immunization shots, and so many of them were knocked down by the fever.

"We can't show sick children to their future parents. We have to wait until they get better. Our orphanage is no heaven. Who-ever is not strong enough dies. Our facility is poor, as you can see. One caretaker has to look after more than twenty infants. And every day we have newborns thrown at our door. All female except for a few deformed males. So many with handicaps or mental illness . . . We just can't do it all."

"Is Little Rabbit all right?" I asked.

"We got her yesterday. She seemed to be fine."

I demanded to see Little Rabbit. The headmistress picked up the keys and then changed her mind. She said, "I'm sorry, but I don't want to lose my job."

I ran to the train station with the last of my strength. The station looked like an animal pen with straw everywhere. The conductor told me that all the tickets had sold out days ago. I asked about a seat in cargo. Seeing me coated with mud, his eyes showed sympathy. He said he wanted to help, but it was not legal because the car was designed to transport animals, not humans. I stuffed fifty yuan in his hand and he hid me in the pig carriage.

By six o'clock in the morning I was on a moving train with pigs. I was back in Shanghai by noon.

When I got off the train, I went straight to the American consulate. I realized that I must have looked crazy when the guard saw me and immediately put his hand on the gun in his belt. I showed the guard my passport and the useless certificate of adoption. The guard let me in.

One of the assistants to the consul general came out and looked carefully at the certificate as I explained the situation. He asked me to wait and went back into his office. I heard him making phone calls. He came out and asked me to come back the next day.

I couldn't sleep. I still smelled of pig shit from the train. My parents stayed up with me. They wanted to know when I would be able to leave for America so they could start preparing. I yelled at them and told them to go to sleep and leave me alone. I said I might not be going at all.

My nerves were tight and my thinking circled the same spot: How could I go without Little Rabbit? How could I tell Katherine that Little Rabbit was someone else's daughter now? I sat by the window waiting for the day to dawn.

At seven-thirty I was the first one in line outside the consulate gate.

I was taken in to see the consul general, who asked me to explain again how Katherine had adopted Little Rabbit. I told him everything I knew, including how I faked the papers in order to place Little Rabbit with a nanny near Elephant Fields so I could take care of her on Katherine's behalf. The consul began to make phone calls.

My heart pounded loudly and I felt strange speaking English with an American official. The phone on his desk rang, and the consul asked me if I'd like to speak with Katherine.

I couldn't move. I sat still in my chair and thought I hadn't understood him correctly. He repeated the question and passed me the receiver.

I stood up, trembling. I heard a voice on the other end calling, "Hello! Hello!" It was Katherine's voice.

I told her what had happened, but I couldn't explain about the forgery. I couldn't be sure the phone wasn't bugged. She told me not to worry, that the consul was going to mail her a copy of the original certificate of adoption, and she would contact the authorities from America.

"Please act fast, Katherine," I said. "This is China. Any minute things could change . . ."

"I know that very well, Zebra," she said. "Now go and take care of Little Rabbit. You'll hear from me soon."

I went back to Elephant Fields. I put all my belongings into a plastic bag. I was off again. I hitchhiked a ride on a tractor to the orphanage to be with Little Rabbit.

The headmistress told me that Little Rabbit's case was "in dispute," which meant no one was allowed to see Little Rabbit.

I didn't know what "in dispute" meant: Had my forgery provoked a criminal investigation? Did it signal the involvement of the U.S. consulate? Or was it just the authorities' way of making Little Rabbit disappear in order to reject Katherine?

During the day, I waited outside the headmistress's office, begging and threatening her to let me see Little Rabbit, hoping my pleas would exhaust her and make her give in. At night I slept in a villager's straw cabin. I was running out of Katherine's money and was preparing myself for hardship.

After two days I bought information from the doorman of the orphanage and learned that Little Rabbit had caught the #2 disease and was running a high fever. She had just been sent to a local hospital emergency room.

I rushed to the hospital. The emergency room was filled with sick children. There were no doctors or nurses around. The beds were arranged in rows. The children seemed half dead.

I found Little Rabbit stuck with intravenous needles. Her face was colorless. I held up my hand to her mouth and could hardly feel her breath.

A nurse came in at midday carrying two baskets and changed the IV bottles for each child. She hurried off as quickly as she came.

No one visited these children.

Little Rabbit opened her eyes halfway. She recognized me but was not able to talk. Her red eyes made her look like a real rabbit.

Her lips cracked like potato chips. She was too weak to move her eyelids. By early evening a doctor came by and told me that Little Rabbit had been drifting in and out of consciousness since she'd arrived.

"We'll see," the doctor said.

I guarded Little Rabbit and fed her thin porridge whenever she was able to swallow. The sick, motionless children around me stared straight at the white ceiling. The innocent and helpless look in their eyes made me feel ashamed for not being able to help them. They couldn't understand why they were made to feel such pain, but when I looked in their eyes, I saw only acceptance.

Every day I hitchhiked rides on tractors from the hospital to the town post office, waiting for mail from Katherine. One rainy afternoon the driver lost control while making a turn by a narrow bridge. The driver and I were thrown in the river. In midair the only thing I thought about was protecting my passport, which was carefully wrapped in wax paper in my chest pocket.

When I resurfaced and found my passport was safe, I didn't even notice the pain in my body. I helped the villagers lift the driver out of the water. He'd broken one of his legs. It could very well have been you, Zebra, I thought.

After a week in the hospital Little Rabbit was getting worse. The hospital had primitive medical equipment, beds were made of bamboo, the towels were mud-colored, and the floors were dirty. Little Rabbit slept most of the time.

Time passed slowly. Early one morning, as I walked along a foggy riverbank, I realized that my life had reached the point where I knew that I would never give up, even if I failed to make it to America. I would not give up. And that was all I expected of myself. I was very happy with this discovery. When I got back to the hospital, I looked at myself in the restroom mirror. I laughed at my reflection. The mirror showed a typical northern Chinese peasant. She had dusty hair that stuck out like a wild plant. She had dark brown skin with heavy cheeks like steamed breads. Her eyes sank in her head like two fish whispering nose to nose. Her nose was a potato. She didn't look afraid. She looked a little silly, but confident and proud.

Ten days after I got back from Shanghai, a telegram came. I showed my passport to the post office clerk and he passed me the green envelope. I was afraid it might be bad news. Maybe Katherine sent the wire to say that she had tried and failed and decided to give in to fate. I tore it open.

I took out the telegram. The characters appeared blurred, then gradually came into focus.

US CONGRESSMAN SPOKE UP FOR ME IN BEIJING. PROBLEM SOLVED. VISAS, IMMIGRATION PAPERS, AND TICKETS AWAIT YOU AT CONSULATE. WILL MEET YOU AND THE CHILD AT THE AIRPORT. LOVE, K.

An extraordinary silence ran through the space of my mind, and I exhaled.

Little Rabbit opened her eyes slowly. She looked up at me. Touching my cheek with her little fingers, she asked, "*Zhe-shi-shi-me?*" What's this?

I waved the telegram at her.

"Mama?"

I nodded.

"Is Mama coming back for me?" Little Rabbit's red eyes widened, her eyebrows knotted as she stared at me, waiting for my reply. Before I could open my mouth, her focus faded and she slid away.

I took her little blue and purple hands, bruised by needles.

The line on the electrocardiograph drew the irregular patterns of her heartbeat.

A round-faced doctor came in and checked her pulse.

"Are you the mother?" he asked, his eyes on his watch.

"Yes."

"She's grabbing hold of herself. She's fighting hard. I think she's going to pull through."

Outside the room, nurses were carrying out a stretcher with a little body wrapped in a white sheet.

No crying, only the sound of footsteps on concrete ground.

"Tomorrow," the doctor said, and threw me a smile as he walked away.

My tears choked me silently. I took out Katherine's Walkman and covered my ears with the headphones.

READ MORE IN PENGUIN

In every corner of the world, on every subject under the sun, Penguin represents quality and variety – the very best in publishing today.

For complete information about books available from Penguin – including Puffins, Penguin Classics and Arkana – and how to order them, write to us at the appropriate address below. Please note that for copyright reasons the selection of books varies from country to country.

In the United Kingdom: Please write to *Dept. EP, Penguin Books Ltd, Bath Road, Harmondsworth, West Drayton, Middlesex UB7 0DA*

In the United States: Please write to *Consumer Sales, Penguin USA, P.O. Box 999, Dept. 17109, Bergenfield, New Jersey 07621-0120*. VISA and MasterCard holders call 1-800-253-6476 to order Penguin titles

In Canada: Please write to *Penguin Books Canada Ltd, 10 Alcorn Avenue, Suite 300, Toronto, Ontario M4V 3B2*

In Australia: Please write to *Penguin Books Australia Ltd, P.O. Box 257, Ringwood, Victoria 3134*

In New Zealand: Please write to *Penguin Books (NZ) Ltd, Private Bag 102902, North Shore Mail Centre, Auckland 10*

In India: Please write to *Penguin Books India Pvt Ltd, 706 Eros Apartments, 56 Nehru Place, New Delhi 110 019*

In the Netherlands: Please write to *Penguin Books Netherlands bv, Postbus 3507, NL-1001 AH Amsterdam*

In Germany: Please write to *Penguin Books Deutschland GmbH, Metzlerstrasse 26, 60594 Frankfurt am Main*

In Spain: Please write to *Penguin Books S. A., Bravo Murillo 19, 1° B, 28015 Madrid*

In Italy: Please write to *Penguin Italia s.r.l., Via Felice Casati 20, I–20124 Milano*

In France: Please write to *Penguin France S. A., 17 rue Lejeune, F–31000 Toulouse*

In Japan: Please write to *Penguin Books Japan, Ishikiribashi Building, 2–5–4, Suido, Bunkyo-ku, Tokyo 112*

In Greece: Please write to *Penguin Hellas Ltd, Dimocritou 3, GR–106 71 Athens*

In South Africa: Please write to *Longman Penguin Southern Africa (Pty) Ltd, Private Bag X08, Bertsham 2013*

READ MORE IN PENGUIN

A CHOICE OF FICTION

Asta's Book Barbara Vine

In 1905, Asta and her husband Rasmus came to East London from Denmark with their two little boys. Over seventy years later, Asta's diaries are published . . . 'Barbara Vine has once again done her readers proud . . . for a good, absorbing, well-told story, you could hardly better the unveiling of Asta's secret' – *Sunday Times*

Peerless Flats Esther Freud

Lisa has high hopes for her first year in London. She is sixteen and ambitious to become more like her sister Ruby. For Ruby has cropped hair, a past, and a rockabilly boyfriend whose father is in prison. 'Freud sounds out as a clear, attractive voice in the literary hubbub' – *Observer*

One of the Family Monica Dickens

At 72, Chepstow Villas lives the Morley family; Leonard, the Assistant Manager of Whiteley's, his gentle wife Gwen, 'new woman' daughter Madge and son Dicky. Into their comfortable Edwardian world comes a sinister threat of murder and a charismatic stranger who will change their lives forever. 'It is the contrasts that Dickens depicts so rivetingly . . . she captures vividly the gradual blurring of social divisions during the last days of the Empire' – *Daily Mail*

Varying Degrees of Hopelessness Lucy Ellman

'Funny and furious . . . what the author is interested in is the hopelessness of life. Her merry little novel is a vehicle for disgust. Lucy Ellman is clever, and very angry' – *The Times*. 'An irresistible cocktail of satire, slapstick and tenderness' – *Cosmopolitan*

The Killjoy Anne Fine

Nobody has ever treated Ian Laidlay in a natural way. Presented with his hideous facial scars, everyone he meets falls back on distant courtesy to hide pity or disgust or shock. But then someone laughs . . . 'A wonderful and original piece of work . . . a horror story which rings absolutely true' – Alan Sillitoe

A CHOICE OF FICTION

The Battle for Christabel Margaret Forster

Rowena wants a baby. What she doesn't want is the baby's father. Yet five years after the birth of Christabel, Rowena is dead, tragically killed in a climbing accident. The battle for Christabel has begun ... 'Poignant, impeccably written ... especially heart-rending because it is so believable' – *Company*

Cleopatra's Sister Penelope Lively

'A fluent, funny, ultimately moving romance in which lovers share centre stage with Lively's persuasive meditations on history and fate ... a book of great charm with a real intellectual resonance at its core' –*The New York Times Book Review*

A Family Romance Anita Brookner

Paul and Henrietta Manning and their solitary, academic daughter Jane have nothing in common with Dolly, widow of Henrietta's brother. But when all Dolly and Jane have left is each other, they discover that history and family create closer ties than friendship ever could. 'This small history unfolds slowly, with delicious wit or bitter pathos, and finally with a marvellous, lingering human resonance' – *Sunday Express*

A Rather English Marriage Angela Lambert

Roy, a retired milkman, and Reggie, a former RAF Squadron-Leader, are widowed on the same day. To assuage their grief, the vicar arranges for Roy to move in with Reggie as his unpaid manservant. To their surprise, they form a strange alliance, based on obedience, need and the strangeness of single life.

The Girl Who Trod on a Loaf Kathryn Davis

'Davis writes of a love between equals that still has tragic modulations. This is the real thing, caught in a language that hovers enticingly between the laconic and the poetic ... this is a novel with secrets, one that repays work, and its prose is exquisitely rhythmic and open-ended' – *Independent*

READ MORE IN PENGUIN

A CHOICE OF FICTION

The Collected Stories William Trevor

Whether they portray the vagaries of love, the bitter pain of loss and regret or the tragic impact of violence upon ordinary lives, these superb stories reveal the insight, subtle humour and unrivalled artistry that make William Trevor the contemporary master of the form.

The Complete Enderby Anthony Burgess

Comprising *Inside Mr Enderby*, *Enderby Outside*, *The Clockwork Testament* and *Enderby's Dark Lady*, these dazzling comic entertainments are a celebration of Burgess's irrepressible creation. 'Ferociously funny and wildly, verbally inventive' – *The Times*

Sugar Cane Paul Bailey

'Bailey has captured two remarkable voices, of a woman who comes to love a young man with maternal solicitude, and of the boy himself, an outcast within his own family . . . A powerful, painful and evocative novel . . . written with such feeling that it makes the reader laugh and weep' – *Spectator*

Dr Haggard's Disease Patrick McGrath

'The reader is compellingly drawn into Dr Haggard's life as it begins to unfold through episodic flashbacks . . . This is the story of a love affair that goes terribly wrong . . . It is a beautiful story, impressively told, with a restraint and a grasp of technicality that command belief, and a lyricism that gives the description of the love affair the sort of epic quality rarely found these days' – *The Times*

A Place I've Never Been David Leavitt

'Wise, witty and cunningly fuelled by narrative . . . another high calibre collection by an unnervingly mature young writer' – *Sunday Times* 'Leavitt can make a world at a stroke and people it with convincing characters . . . humane, touching and beautifully written' – *Observer*

READ MORE IN PENGUIN

A CHOICE OF FICTION

The Lying Days   Nadine Gordimer

Raised in the conservative mining town of Atherton, South Africa, Helen Shaw, seventeen, longs to escape from the sterile environment that has shaped her parents' rigid attitudes and threatens to corrode her own fragile values. At last, finding the courage and maturity to stand alone, she leaves behind the 'lying days' of her youth.

The Eye in the Door   Pat Barker

'Barker weaves fact and fiction to spellbinding effect, conjuring up the vastness of the First World War through its chilling impact on the minds of the men who endured it ... a startlingly original work of fiction ... it extends the boundaries not only of the anti-war novel, but of fiction generally' – *Sunday Telegraph*

Strange Pilgrims   Gabriel García Márquez

The twelve stories in this collection by the Nobel prizewinner chronicle the surreal, haunting 'journeys' of Latin Americans in Europe. 'Márquez's genius is for the physical. Characters urinate, devour songbird stew; old people remember their youthful lovemaking ... It is this spirit of generous desire that fills his work' – *The Times*

Millroy the Magician   Paul Theroux

A magician of baffling talents, a vegetarian and a health fanatic with a mission to change the food habits of America, Millroy has the power to heal, and to hypnotize. 'Fresh and unexpected ... this very accomplished, confident book is among his best' – *Guardian*

The House of Doctor Dee   Peter Ackroyd

When Matthew Palmer inherits an old house in Clerkenwell he feels himself to have become a part of its past. Compelled to probe its mysteries, he discovers to his horror and curiosity that the previous owner was a practitioner of black magic. 'A good old-fashioned spine-chiller of a ghost story ... which will also be taken as a serious modern novel' – *The Times*

READ MORE IN PENGUIN

A CHOICE OF FICTION

Crazy in Alabama Mark Childress

Way down South – in Industry, Alabama – 1965 was the year the orphan Peejoe discovered it wasn't sage to treat black people the same way you treated whites. Perhaps it was around the same time his Aunt Lucille arrived with her husband's head in a Tupperware box – he never could be sure . . . 'A truly wild, uplifting book' – *Time Out*

Memories of the Ford Administration John Updike

'Vintage Updike and a cracking good novel . . . Updike is always a polished performer. No other writer has explored the muddle of modern America with such honesty, clarity and plain good humour' – *Sunday Express*

The Children of Men P. D. James

'As taut, terrifying and ultimately convincing as anything in the dystopian genre. It is at once a piercing satire on our cosseted, faithless and trivially self-indulgent society and a most tender love story' – *Daily Mail*

The Only Problem Muriel Spark

Harvey Gotham had abandoned his beautiful wife Effie on the *autostrada* in Italy. Now, nearly a year later, ensconced in France where he is writing a monograph on the Book of Job, his solitude is interrupted by Effie's sister. Suddenly Harvey finds himself longing for the unpredictable pleasure's of Effie's company. But she has other ideas. 'One of this century's finest creators of the comic-metaphysical entertainment' – *The New York Times*

Collected Stories Beryl Bainbridge

Women in fox furs, not-quite-travelling salesmen, the twilight zone of genteel hotels and lodging houses – this is quintessential Bainbridge territory. This volume also contains the novella *Filthy Lucre*, written when the author was thirteen.

READ MORE IN PENGUIN

A CHOICE OF FICTION

Sacred Hunger Barry Unsworth

'Unsworth's theme is human rivalry; his subject is the slave trade of the mid-eighteenth century . . . *Sacred Hunger* is a tremendous performance. Not the least of its achievements is the sense of blood, guts and hurricanes existing side by side with an imaginatively realized interior life' – *Sunday Times*

The Vicar of Sorrows A. N. Wilson

'Hard to resist . . . scoring at least three unequivocal triumphs – as a bleakly funny portrait of male mid-life breakdown, as a serious piece of anti-theology and as a satire on Anglicanism' – *Daily Telegraph*

Mayday Jonathan Lynn

'A very funny, insightful and intelligent book and a taut thriller which will keep you turning the pages right to the surprising end' – Eric Idle. '*Mayday* is not a cry for help – it is a yelp for joy. Lynn's movie moguls, mysteries and mishaps leap straight off the page' – Maureen Lipman

Cal Bernard Mac Laverty

Springing out of the fear and violence of Ulster, Cal is a haunting love story in a land where tenderness and innocence can only flicker briefly in the dark. 'A gripping political thriller and a formidable fictional triumph' – *Observer*

Bridie and Finn Harry Cauley

Bridie and Finn are like chalk and cheese. She's motherless and loquacious. He's the quiet type, with a crooked leg from birth. And they become the best of friends. True to the unpredictable twists and turns of life, *Bridie and Finn* creates a hugely memorable mosaic of human relationships.

READ MORE IN PENGUIN

A CHOICE OF FICTION

Body of Glass Marge Piercy

'Outstanding . . . I have not read a more disturbing or moving novel about artificial intelligence since Mary Shelley's *Frankenstein* . . . It elevates its author to the pantheon of *haute* SF alongside Doris Lessing and Ursula Le Guin' – *Financial Times*

The Madness of a Seduced Woman Susan Fromberg Schaeffer

In her search for all-consuming, perfect love, Agnes Dempster, a beautiful young woman in turn-of-the-century Vermont, becomes infatuated with a man who, frightened by her intensity, betrays her. 'I can't remember a single other character in fiction with whom I have ever identified more . . . A great many women have tried to write *the* feminist novel. *This* is the novel they've been trying to write' – Margaret Forster

Now You Know Michael Frayn

'A constantly witty writer . . . Frayn's book can best be compared to a pin: it is small, shiny, sharp. Its impact will, one hopes, prick people into examining or re-examining one of the most teasing moral problems of our times' – *Spectator*

Brazzaville Beach William Boyd

'Hope Clearwater lives on an African beach reassessing the complicated, violent and tragic events which have occurred in her life. How much has she been responsible? How could she have forseen the dangers? . . . Boyd is a brilliant storyteller . . . a most serious book which stretches, tantalizes and delights' – *Financial Times*

Emily's Shoes Dermot Bolger

'A novel of enormous ambition, an attempt to create a folk history for those whose dark sexuality has banished them into the underworld of their own country . . . a serious and provocative work of fiction' – *Sunday Times*